The Last Three Minutes

Anyway Books® Works by John Nicholas Datesh

*The Girl in the Coyote Coat (novel)**
*A Need Apart (novel)**
**Same book, different title*
The Body in the Bog
The Last Three minutes
The Nightmare Machine (novel)
The Janus Murder (novel)
The Moscow Tape (novel)

You Could Call it a Christmas Story (short)
The Pro Station (short)
The Final Equation (short)
Reruns ad Infinitum (short)
The Very First Blog Posts of All Time
(on the blog EmptyGlassFull.com

The Last Three Minutes

an Anyway Books® novel by

John Nicholas Datesh

Published by
Loiseau Media

The Last Three Minutes

an Anyway Books® novel by

John Nicholas Datesh

An *Anyway Books* Novel published
by Loiseau Media/Anyway Books
ISBN 978-1-940227-13-9

John Nicholas Datesh is a
pseudonym of John Nicholas Datesh, Jr.

This novel, its characters, their thoughts,
actions, and dialogue, are fictitious.

The Last Three Minutes

Introduction

June 2013

Comforting as the belief may have been, Julian Cochran did not have Leigh's faith in comebacks. For him, there was no *Other* Side, no *In Between.*

Leigh is dead. Period, amen.

Screw that last part.

Yet, right then, he had some serious explaining to do.

So, how the...

The *how* did not matter to him. If it was there, Leigh's app was there, on his new phone. That mattered.

He had not seen it download. He knew Leigh's app was not in the Google Play Store. He had looked for it dozens of times, maybe hundreds. It was not in any virtual store or in any of their Cloud accounts. It had not been in anything, nothing outside of their house. Until–

Leigh?

Before the app's spontaneous appearance, Julian had been sitting in his office, absently watching Android apps download to his new Moto X. Unlike his NorAm Logistics co-workers, Julian had replaced the company-issued Blackberry using his own money. He had plenty, thanks to his best man Frank Leonard's insistence on an over-supply of life insurance – through Frank's broker father, Ben – and he refused to let NorAm buy him the new smartphone. Besides, he was not sure how much longer he would be there.

Julian was grateful to NorAm and his immediate superiors. Though his bosses knew he did not need the job, they knew he *needed* the job. NorAm no longer needed Julian, but, even in a fog, he was the only gifted logistics manager they had.

For the six months leading to Leigh's August death, Julian telecommuted most days. His job was all computer and phone work, anyway. After her death, NorAm let him continue telecommuting for another couple months. Eventually, he had graduated to three short days in-office. Two weeks before he had begun loading the Moto X, Julian had begun normal hours.

Despite zero improvements in his performance, he valued the pretense of normality, the logic of shipping product from point A to point B and, maybe, C through Z.

Still, he had not truly come back. They all assumed he never would. That dismal fact had made coming to work liberating. The false sense of freedom ended when a too familiar Father Time icon, complete with scythe, popped up onto the Moto X screen.

And the wait is over.

That icon, representing Leigh's egg timer app, did not belong there. The app certainly did not belong.

It did not surprise him so much as irk him. "Open your own damned self!" he said aloud.

The app did just that, blackening the display for a moment. Then, it flashed Leigh's dancing egg animation and played one of her app's short playlist, *Open All Night,* by Bruce Springsteen.

No Offense, Bruce.

Julian tried and missed the tiny *Mute* icon twice before he expanded the display enough to quiet Springsteen. He glanced out his open door for reactions.

No one so much as cocked an ear. Apparently, a bubble of grief was soundproof.

He should have suspended the whole egg timer app, but he did not. He rarely did. He could have removed the intrusive app from his computers, but he could not find it. Apps were supposed to download to run. He had searched. The truth was he would not have deleted it had he found it. He and the Egg had a *thing*.

It is Leigh's.

And neither of us can dance a lick.

Leigh had not had a mean streak in her. She *had* designed the app to torture him, but only to make a point, playfully, one with a very practical purpose. That had been fine because Julian had loved her sense of humor.

What had just happened shook him, badly. It did not scare him. It was far worse than that.

He caught it in long face reflected briefly in the Moto's shiny screen.

At demented look.

Crazy with hope.

Julian stood up and put the Moto X in his back pocket. He walked out of the office, ignoring whatever he had brought in with him. He walked down an aisle of cubes, not looking at their denizens. Nobody watched him, but they knew where he was going and the topic on his mind: Julian had tried to live, normally live, without Leigh. That foolish experiment was over.

He entered the open office of NorAm's general manager. He did not show her the crazy dancing egg or unmute the song. He did not acknowledge the hope he continued to resist.

As he settled into the elevator for the last time, Julian gave in, with a solemn promise to retract the thought later:

Assuming neither he nor the Cloud was insane, then the Cloud had not downloaded the app all by itself.

Leigh had.

Chapter One

July 2013

For some time, Julian held the beautiful, blond angel at eye level and dared the blue eyes to return the favor. He was six-foot two, with hazel/green eyes and brown hair. The angel – two-foot, not counting the wings and halo – seemed indifferent and it's eyes were...

The eyes were close to that particular blue color of Leigh's. It was why it had been her favorite from the moment she saw it.

Leigh's blue was not quite *sky*. It was a both lighter and a little duskier than that, deeper, Julian's preferred shade of blue.

"I know you're not in there. So why am I doing this?"

He knew the stand-off had reached one minute and forty-three seconds.

I don't need your app anymore.

Over eleven to late months, Leigh's app of a legacy had trained him to track time in minutes and their subparts. Julian had never been interested or capable of such accuracy, but it had been drilled into him by a dancing egg and a bunch of songs.

While his mind kept track, he tried to blank out the lyrics of the song playing upstairs on any or all his devices, including his desktop computer, his phone, his tablet, and her laptop. It took too much effort not to think the words whether they played aloud or not.

The eyes glinted. He straightened, blocking the lamp, deadening the effect. The gold silk gown, too, lost its shimmer.

"I tried, Leigh," he said, placing her favorite between two lesser versions on the mantel, as closely to her exact placement as he could. "Besides, in theory, angels start out as angels. You were just a girl."

Julian winced. The moment passed, without a lightning strike. Leigh disliked that expression.

"Just?" she would have asked. "Just?"

"I meant *especially* and *heavenly*."

"Not yet, but give me a month."

Leigh had been especially funny about her looming death.

She joked about it and about angels and about life after death, all of which she had accepted, even as Julian had not. The believer-non-believer sharing only a queen mattress made humor a better choice than argument. Too, they may have had a problem figuring out how best to argue.

As adamant as Julian had always been, he had wished, often, that he had believed. Then, even only then, would have been nice. Every day since, too, but that was just greedy.

Julian stood in their living room, his left shoe tapping a deep cardboard box. To him, that carton was supposed to host the splendid winged craft-work for eternity. Or until the next neighborhood flea market.

Among the things Julian reluctantly believed in was bad karma. He tried to sell himself on being merely sentimental, but the idea of banishing Leigh's avatar to the depths – just the idea – had spooked for months.

"It's a damned nice cellar," he said aloud. It sounded so hollow, even explained to doll-spirits, that he augmented it with the penultimate argument: "If it is good enough for Lily..."

Lily, as blond as Leigh, was just... *especially* as dead and for longer. Leigh, herself, had approved the spot for Lily's urn in the basement. She had been careful of its location, relying on her uncanny knack of the aesthetic use of space.

"Leigh," he had said. "It's the cellar."

"I know you don't care, but it has to look right to me."

Julian may not have cared, but, as usual, the urn's spot *did* look right to him. Just as all the annoying angels looked as he viewed the living room. Some were grouped, others solitary, but the space looked perfect.

He nudged the box toward the corner of the Sea Foam carpet, where three other boxes waited to ferry all the angels surrounding him to a better place, a very pleasant neighborhood flea market.

Leigh's unerring eye had been right, he thought: Almost everything, including cardboard, went with Sea Foam. The paint did and on every wall. Leigh had seized on *Clam Cay* before she had seen the sample. "The perfect sounding off-white for the carpet," she had claimed, disingenuously.

Julian knew Leigh's *signs* when he saw two. Since their first Caribbean vacation, they had talked about living on an island someday, and she had not given up on half of that dream.

He jumped when he heard the synthetic voice, say, "Ding! Oh, Julian," before *Dream Baby*, by Hootie and the Blowfish, started. At least, he mused, it was not Olivia Newton-John's *Hopelessly Devoted*.

Hopelessly Wacko was the aptest term for a guy who could not suspend Leigh's time-counting app, the one with an array of three-minute songs. Leigh had designed the app to *torture* him for being time-challenged.

If only she had known.

The source of the voice was not Leigh's – she had tried that – but, thankfully, she had made it so appealing that he found it comforting. Not that Leigh had intended him to keep running the app for a year. Its purpose, too, had expired.

He planned to face that after he dealt with the angels.

Julian kicked the angel box into the air and ran for the stairs to pause the music. Computers were real. Computer apps, he could control if he wanted.

The run stopped cold at the bottom of the staircase. His mind raced up the stairs without him, still determined to win.

It would be crazy if it happened all the time.

He did not wait for the *mental* run to end before he forced a foot onto the first step. He did not hesitate again until he reached the narrow table set in a windowed alcove between the two upstairs hall closets. One of his favorite photos of Leigh – complete with Lily – smiled at him between the backs of two more angels. Julian had re-purposed them to watch over the back yard. They did not look *right*, but he had to live with them.

"If you can't box them, use them," his friend Frank had suggested. "They are cheaper and scarier than an ADT sign."

They did look freaky as hell from the back yard. He hadn't seen a raccoon in months.

To Julian's right was what passed, in small colonials, for a master bedroom, to the left two bedrooms. The smaller of the two was an office, lately home to both of their computers. After the sixth month, Julian had progressed to calling their master bedroom *The Bedroom*, but their computers were another story.

In the face of his stubbornly halfhearted effort, Leigh's laptop had remained *Leigh's laptop* in name and spirit. Perhaps, if it had not been a shade of blond... but that was why it had become Leigh's laptop in the first place. She had picked it from a dozen competitors at Best Buy, much as she had once picked Lily from a *rescue* litter.

Leigh had not been vain about her fine hair, but she had been keen on *signs.* She had brushed past Julian and a slickly black ultrabook, with a dual-function–

"Oh, sorry, Julian." No one had bothered to open the very light tan, spec-challenged notebook. Leigh did. "She's the one."

At the time, Julian had silently queried the sales rep who shrugged. "We only that. The floor model. I'm surprised we ordered even this one."

Leigh had picked up and hugged the laptop. "I'm not."

To her credit, Leigh had not given the laptop a name like *Lola* or *Lana.* She had chosen a designation instead: Leigh's laptop.

"It is a notebook. We don't call them–"

She had given him her tolerantly disappointed look. "Alliteration is less work, Julian."

"And yet you married me."

"I wasn't thinking about work, at the time."

Whatever it had been called, the notebook had become and remained wholly hers. Julian had used it on occasion and in the last months had taken to talking to it. He felt it was less embarrassing to hear himself talking to Leigh's laptop most of the time than to Leigh.

Besides, he judged its microphone above average and its emanations – electromagnetic though they were – comfortably real.

Julian stood over his desk. The anarchy of the office contrasted with the rest of the house. Nothing ever in its proper place, it had lain outside of Leigh's purview. If she had become a poltergeist, she would have started with the office.

The desktop monitor was angled to leave space immediately to the right for Leigh's laptop. A Galaxy tablet sat on an inkjet printer/scanner on the monitor's left. Each screen showed identical count-down clocks and he looked at them back and forth. When the count hit :28 he sat down. There was nothing magical about the count, but it gave him time to mute the computer and the tablet. He turned the tablet over. He then clicked off *auto* on the laptop and desktop apps.

Lucky them, he thought.

The clocks were not alone on their screens. Below each, a tall, narrow shot glass slowly drained of a clear liquid. Leigh's idea of an hourglass. Beside and around the glass, there danced an animated, tan-colored egg. The egg had Mrs. Potato Head-style eyes and nose but an all too clearly Smiley Face mouth and well-drawn legs. It moved as well as could be expected, lacking a waist. Hootie's was not a dance song, but it was exactly three minutes long. Julian kept watching the liquid, what he knew to be small-v vodka, a generic.

Leigh had preferred the Grey Goose with her Vicodin, but "I economized consonants for the app."

"Ding! Oh, Julian," said the mysterious voice from Leigh's laptop. The eggs had already landed atop their respective shooters, their bottom ends too big for the openings. The legs swung once more and stopped. The music stopped.

Blessed Silence.

Play icons appeared.

She had given him some *control.*

Leigh had programmed in random play for the songs, although lately, it had seemed less so. Still, Julian had no idea which would come next and internally heard a cacophony of songs in anticipation.

He hit the *Play* icon on the laptop. All the eggs – including the tablet's he knew – leaped off the shot glasses and start swaying to *Time is on My Side* by the Rolling Stones.

Three minutes was supposed to be the perfect length for a song, but with the animation, it could seem like a long time.

Sometimes three minutes seemed like forever… sometimes not.

The thousandth plus rerun should not have elicited the spoken "Very ironic, Leigh," but Julian usually said it, anyway.

Leigh had truly believed she would hear him.

"Bet you ten bucks you can't."

Eleven months in and he still waited for half a tick for a meow-backed "Leave it for me at the front gate."

Chapter Two

June 2010

Leigh knew it was foolhardy to believe it, but she just saw it that way in her mind. She had always believed that she and Lily would reunite on the other side and, together, they would watch over Julian.

She had never expected Lily to go first. She had certainly never imagined that she would be the one to kill her sweet Lily.

Yet that was where her love and her laptop *first* led her.

She fell in love with Lily, faster than with Julian by seconds or weeks, depending upon whether Julian or Leigh, respectively, was narrating their first encounter.

The Humane Society had three dozen *rooms* arrayed in its *Cat Dormitory.* From each cage, one or more anxious felines eyed Leigh and Julian as Becky, volunteer fresh from her own dorm, led them inside a room the color of mid-summer grass and unnervingly quiet.

"How much Benadryl do you go through?" Julian asked.

Becky swiped her right index finger over her clipboard before realizing it was not her new iPad. She got halfway through a sigh before–

"That's her," Leigh said. She pointed to a flat-faced fur-ball as if she had just picked out her favorite cousin in a mosh pit.

"This kitty is named Lily," Becky said, without a glance at her roster. Everyone at the shelter knew Lily. "She's a little over three?" Beck said, implying the age was negotiable. "But she's had all her shots."

At the sound of the *L name*. Leigh shot Julian a *See, but don't comment* look.

"She's wonderful. Isn't she Julian? Can I hold her?"

Julian winced as he saw Becky prepare to retrieve Lily from her second-level cage. It was not the inevitability acquisition but the elbow-length leather gloves that had him looking for a *printed* sign, one that would say "hold animals at your own risk." He saw it back by the door.

Becky reached down toward Lily, murmuring sweet nothings. Lily rewarded the soft words with a swipe of a paw, lots of teeth and a diaphragm-flexing hiss. Becky let Lily repeat the gestures. "She's front-declawed."

Julian asked, "When will you tell her?"

Lily sank purring into Leigh's arms.

Once the shock wore off, Becky relaxed and sketched Lily's history as a fluffy blond three-time loser. Lilly had been abandoned as a kitten, adopted and declawed and returned. A college girl adopted her but returned her to the Humane Society, because, as her new boyfriend put it, Lily was "way too fucking feisty" for her own good. The staff had largely given up on matching her with a suitable owner.

Leigh left the form-signing to Julian because her hands were buried in fur.

Lily's front paws had surgically lost their claws, but Lily used them as if scalpels had been sewn in by mistake. Leigh fed her Cat Chow Indoor Formula, all of which she digested well except the title. Every day, she sat by the door, awaiting Leigh's arrival home from work. She did the same for Julian. She followed her routine because she loved Leigh and because she knew Julian would eventually give her a gap to shoot. Even when Leigh was too sick to move, Lily would take a break from her side in hopes Julian would forget how quick a cat could be.

Julian did not love Lily, but he loved Leigh, and he respected Lily. They were both tenacious and tougher than they looked. Lily had helped comfort Leigh through her first round of chemotherapy, far more than the increasing population of angels or even Julian had. Lily had the advantage of being full-time, a fact that had made Julian feel better about his ranking.

Caregiver or not, Lily's still had a yen to stay in fighting trim, primarily to punch out a backyard raccoon whenever possible. She stubbornly ignored Julian's advice – "You don't bring a spoon to a fork fight"–and kept at it when she could steal an opportunity.

No unbeaten streak lasted forever.

~ ~ ~

Julian downed some Sam Adams and poked at the steaks to juice the flames. Some rain drops sizzled on the open lid of the grill.

Leigh looked sleek in a t-shirt and skinny jeans, just standing and rocking the puff-ball Lily in her arms. It had taken a while for her to recover from *ethereal* and reclining. The two looked wonderfully comical to Julian: One built like a whippet, the other like a Chia Pet. As if she sensed an insult, Lily turned baleful blue eyes toward him. A rumble of thunder preempted her attention and drew a low hiss.

"It's nothing, Lily," Leigh said, reflexively firming her grip. "It's probably for something Julian was thinking about us." She sat down at the porch's bistro table, she had positioned perfectly months before.

"Brain-wave intercepts are NSA territory." He was alert enough to convert his similes. "But I was thinking, you both look very feline. In different species."

When confined indoors, Lily barely acknowledged lightning or thunder. She seemed interested only in whether Leigh was up to a lap-sit. On the porch, however, she kept Thor himself in her sights.

"You should take her in," Julian said. "We're not going to eat out here, in a thunderstorm."

"As soon as I finish this." Leigh's laptop sat on the table, displaying a pdf of an ad page layout. As Leigh's remission took hold, she had begun distance consulting for the ad agency for which she once worked. She lacked the energy for a commute let alone full-time work. Even at the small size, she could tell the layout was off. It was, after all, destined for small screens. She closed her eyes for a moment then looked back at the screen. She typed some notes into WordPad.

Leigh took a sip of the Chardonnay, typed some notes into her note pop-up and started to smile.

Julian watched the smile. "I didn't know your lips could be *sardonic*."

"And you thought you'd seen me at my; worst." She laughed. "Chalk up another week in Purgatory. I am actually pleased with how far off Cindy's ad looks."

"You're still her boss."

"Supervisor. Her failed mentor, from the look of it. That's another reason I shouldn't feel this way."

Julian shrugged. "Last week, I felt vindicated when one of Glenn's shipments to Costco is three minutes late. He didn't follow my route advice."

Glenn was a NorAm co-worker who routinely vied with Julian for District Logistics Manager of the Month.

"We are both damned–"

A flash lit the sky just ahead of a sharp clap.

"You just had to say–" He stopped as Leigh's glass hit the floor and Lily hurtled past him. "Fuck!"

Leigh had cleared her chair when he said, "Do not even think about it. I'll get her."

Julian returned thirty minutes later, soaking wet. Leigh greeted him on the porch with a flashlight. He flicked on the switch. Nothing happened. He tried again.

She looked wide-eyed and shattered on his third try. Then, she said, "Wait." Her eyes narrowed. "They're in a baggie. Next to the Grey Goose. They last longer."

Julian retrieved the icy batteries, installed them and aimed the light into the yard.

As if in response, a screech sliced through them.

"Oh, shit."

Leigh sighed and went to the screen door. She opened it, turned and opened an eye-level cabinet.

"Good idea," he said, watching her unzip a small plastic zip-bag with faintly pink pills. "Lily will need some Valium."

The Paxil, Ativan, Xanax and Vicodin bottles were up in their bathroom, along with another Valium. Going through surgery and treatment, her doctors had prescribed them all. They had helped but not enough to empty the bottles.

Leigh slender fingers vibrated as they jabbed at the pills. She had switched to plastic bags after her shakes had spewed pills all over the floor a few times. She liked to say she had "pills for every nerve-taxing disorder except irony."

Julian anticipated her next stop. "You may want to save some Grey Goose for the raccoon."

She looked back at him, freezer handle in her grip, anger flaring into her eyes. "Somethings I don't like to share," Leigh said sharply. She jerked the door open and fingered one of the tall cylindrical shot glasses she kept in a frozen line next to the vodka. She took one and slid out the bottle.

The absence left such a lopsided hole, she thought. She shivered, returned the bottle and glass to their spots and slowly closed the door.

"Okay, so fuck the raccoon."

"No," she said. "I'm just wondering which vet ER is open."

~ ~ ~

Eventually, Leigh came to see Lily's death as a blessing. The resignation came first, then a sense of duty. She owed it to Lily to end her suffering. She could not deny, too, that the after-life angle played into her decision.

Even at the moment Lily stopped breathing, Leigh did not blame the raccoon. It was a raccoon, after all, and Lily probably had built up a reputation that drew all the neighborhood's top raccoons.

She did not blame Julian for finding Lily too late. It had already been too late. She did not blame herself for not holding Lily tightly enough, though, given a chance, she would not make that mistake again. Leigh did not blame the ER vet who said he could fix Lily or her own vet, Deandra Jent, who said she could not. Lily had over-treated most of her wounds herself.

Cats had that knack.

Cats' other knack, stoically feigning normality so that humans could fool themselves for months, had Leigh fooled, but not for months. She just could not let Lily go. Her stubborn selfishness surprised and disappointed her.

One day, Julian returned home from work to utter silence. No TV, no person-cat conversation. Finally, he heard Leigh clacking on her laptop in the kitchen. He found her, in her green silk robe, immersed in a website, the table hosting two of the shooter glasses bracketing to a bottle of Valium. It did not look right. No Lily, he realized.

When Leigh failed to react to his entrance, he asked, "Is one of those for me?"

She started, looked at him and slammed the laptop shut. "You scared me half to death, damn it!"

"Not a chance. You're still under warranty," he said, omitting the *five-year* cancer-horizon as a modifier.

"And who's counting?"

Lily's absence was a very bad sign. Julian considered adding a hopeful *Lily, too* but thought better of it.

Leigh looked away. "She's licking her wounds, I think."

"Yeah, well..." Julian picked up the shooters and eyed their dregs in turn. He fetched the Grey Goose and filled both shooters. "Here's to Limited Warranties."

She threw back her vodka. "And somewhat better living through chemistry."

Julian hesitated, evaluating her mood as a notch above glum before he downed the shot.

"Don't look at me like that. This is my favorite afternoon robe." She smiled, sweetly and added, "Because you bought it for me two years ago."

"I knew it would bring out the green in your eyes."

"The sad part is that I would believe you," she replied. "Except I know the blue one was gone by Christmas Eve."

"You couldn't know that."

"You lost track halfway through the Twelve Days," she explained. "You told Frank... So, everyone knew."

"That was not my fault," Julian said, straight-faced. "As a NorAm logistics professional, I knew that kind of inventory shortfall should never happen. Someone else did a bad job, not me."

She did not deliver a clever rejoinder because all she could think was how much his playful inanity help her cope with her own reality. When it came back, she would seriously need that counter-balance.

But for what she had to do next, she realized, Julian – his humor and he, himself – would be just as seriously out-of-place.

~ ~ ~

Perhaps, for Leigh's sake, Lily denied her increasing suffering as long as she could. Finally, the failure of the third-generation antibiotic to neutralize the third infection became too much for Lily. She went into hiding most of the day.

Dr. Jent gave Leigh a link to begin researching pet euthanasia on the internet. It took a full week for Leigh to use the link. Her last day of searching was the scene Julian had interrupted a week earlier. The descriptions of the process had comforted Leigh: Lily would not suffer. Lily's disappearing act had convinced Leigh to make the appointment.

She did not tell Julian about it. He would insist on accompanying her. She tried, but she could not see that as *fitting*. She had laid out the room in her head and could not fit Julian into the scene.

Leigh ignored the kitty carrier. She cradled Lily in her arms into the car and let her stay on her lap for the entire drive to the vet's office. Lily purred, less loudly than usual, but the purring comforted Leigh instead of breaking her down.

Deandra Jent did not keep Leigh and Lily waiting. Against waiting room protocol, Lily overflowed Leigh's narrow lap, into her arms. No one hinted at rule enforcement. Deandra and her staff had agonized nearly as much as Leigh over the purpose of the visit. Once alerted to their arrival, Deandra herself came out of the exam room and took them back inside. She waited until Leigh once again had a lap with Lily on it.

"I'll be back in just a minute. Everything is ready."

Lily had always had white-coat syndrome, and she began to fidget weakly.

Leigh hummed softly, trying to calm the tiny, racing heart. It was not a song, although Leigh wondered if she had unconsciously pirated something. No doubt Julian would have said something about royalties or acoustics, making her laugh or, at least, roll her eyes. That, too, would not have fit.

The four exam rooms shared bad acoustics and warm fawn paint. The color helped the otherwise severe cubes seem inviting, warming even the stainless-steel table tops. The two chairs had more stainless supporting hard plastic seats of muted orange. The walls were decorated with large shots of graceful big cats, serenely dominating savannas, hills or forests. The static images had always fascinated Leigh but had never done a thing for Lily.

All of this, Leigh had seen in her visions of the moment and those to come. It calmed her, and that seemed to affect Lily. The fidgeting stopped.

Through the door, Leigh heard Dr. Jent tell one of her aides, "No. Thank you. Leigh will not let you, anyway."

Leigh knew Deandra really meant: There was no place in the room for witnesses.

Deandra reentered with a stethoscope around her neck and a small metal tray, on which lay a white cloth, three syringes, and an IV set.

Leigh had nixed the single-drug IV method and had bristled at the first mention of cost considerations. Also, Dr. Jent had determined that Lily 's veins were not robust.

"That runs in the family." Leigh had suffered through enough bad IVs in her cancer treatments. "Lily may not freak, but I will." From there, Leigh and Deandra had worked out Lily's custom three-injection process.

Deandra let Lily wave a paw at her as she leaned in to give Lily the Valium shot. "She doesn't give up easily."

"That shot's mostly for me," Leigh said.

They sat in silence for a few minutes before Deandra said, "You didn't tell Julian, I take it."

"No. He is more sensitive than he thinks. I just couldn't see him being here." Leigh felt Lily's heart rate slow a bit as the purring increase slightly. "Julian can be unpredictable about death these days. Lily and I will have to look out for him."

Dr. Jent looked at Lily, but both her eyebrows were raised.

"Don't worry, Dr. Jent. That's an inside joke."

"Okay. How's she doing?"

"She's pretty relaxed." Leigh took a deep breath and sighed it out. "I know I'm just projecting, but I felt Lily was always worried about me. And, lately, about how I would do after she was gone."

"Love fools us, Leigh," Deandra said, gently, "but my experience is that cats don't have that type of feeling... any more than men do." Her voice took on a rasp on the last phrase.

"I'm not sure," Leigh said before she remembered Deandra was twice-divorced at thirty-seven. "About cats, I mean."

"I couldn't help myself."

"Me, either." She kissed Lily's head and looked back at Dr. Jent. "Okay."

Deandra administered the second syringe, a Medetomidine-butorphanol sedating mixture. In only a few minutes, Lily closed her eyes and her heart rate dropped. She kept purring.

"I can bring in Sandy for the IV–"

"No." Leigh could not help but shudder. "God, I hate them, but I'll help if you need me to."

The IV went in without a hitch.

Dr. Jent listened to Lily's heart. "Whenever you are ready."

"How long will it take?"

"She has lost a bit of weight since we first talked, so it will only take a few minutes."

"Okay."

Deandra paused with the syringe in her hand. She had never considered allowing an owner to touch a syringe before and never would again. There was just something so different about Leigh. She gave Leigh the syringe.

Leigh kissed Lily on the head. She looked up, taking in the room. It was as she had seen it. She inserted the syringe into the IV. She depressed the plunger slowly, perfectly. She kissed Lily again and handed over the empty syringe "God, that wasn't as hard as I thought it would be. I could feel how peaceful she is."

"It is something." Deandra took a breath. "You don't have to–"

"No, I will stay until you're sure," Leigh insisted. "She didn't leave me, and I won't leave her."

"She's a very lucky girl."

Leigh continued to stroke Lily, pausing only to brush a tear occasionally.

"So, you still want the cremation?"

"Yes..." She felt and sounded a little dissociated herself. "I think we all should be," she heard herself say.

"I was going out to dinner."

"Oh. Sorry," she said, her eyes widened. "Not today."

They both laughed, parting the pall of tension that had slowly settled on the exam room.

"Her heart is still beating."

"It will for a few minutes, yet."

"She's purring," Leigh said, with a smile. "It's like she likes it."

"Lily was sick. She knew she would not last much longer, Leigh," Deandra said. "You knew that when she started hiding, even from you."

"Yes, I know."

"She feels a lot less pain, less dread. That's for sure."

Leigh nodded and began to wonder what it felt like for Lily, what it *would* feel like. Less dread sounded good.

Minutes passed in outward silence, as Deandra Jent gave Leigh respectful space to mourn. Leigh's soul and her mind were operating independently and, by the time Lily's heart had stopped, Leigh had decided she could do it. She could do it for herself.

Perhaps, she would not be able to do it all, though. Because very likely, she would be too zoned-out or even unconscious to finish it.

Damn, she thought.

"So, Julian, do you love me as much as I loved Lily?"

"More?"

He would be reluctant to diminish her feelings for Lily and would smile when he added, "A little more."

That's a little more *than plenty, Julian.*

She kissed Lily's head one last time and said, "Thank you."

Chapter Three

Pre-2013

The eternal love affair began as more of a blink in April 1996. Leigh and Julian were in their last years at Pittsburgh's Carnegie Mellon University when they first saw each other, in passing. Each caught the other's eye, though Julian never did understand how he caught hers.

Later, Leigh explained that, initially, she spotted what she took for a pained expression worn by an otherwise nice-looking, tallish guy walking by her. There was no room involved and the encounter failed the magical test. She was preparing to hop into the rear a semi-trailer.

When the guy's narrowed eyes noticeably shifted toward her, his expression did not change. He blinked.

"I was blinded. She had this halo," he insisted, a full year later, on their first double date with his housemate Frank and his *pending* fiancée – her accurate words from about a fifth date – Polly Mathis. Because they were Julian's closest friends, the date represented a big step up in the budding relationship.

Polly and Frank had met two years earlier. She was also with Cape Spear Commercial Insurance and a new company policy forced her to take along a numbers-freak of a risk manager to several borderline clients. Her voluptuous appeal, big brown chocolate brown eyes and matching cascading hair got her in every door. She had a carefree air that belied a *canines in neck* tenacity. Polly stole clients from every competitor. She never lost a renewal, either. To her, the only risk in insurance was that some timid nerd would refuse to let sell or renew a policy or overprice the damned thing, which had the same result.

Immediately, she found in Frank an irresistible anti-nerd who treated every number as if he owned it. If he had a problem with her pitch, he worked it out with her over dinner, drinks or... not in office meetings. Right away, they alternated expense accounts and four-slice toasters. Frank was something of a toast addict.

Frank had met Julian in the numbers program at Brown University. They hit it off and ended up rooming together for their last two years. They were both good looking, intelligent and – they seemed to believe – quick witted. Frank was the extrovert of the two, but not so much as to unduly complicate Julian's life. Frank was very particular when selecting the right *type* girl to sell on Julian.

In narrowing his search for business schools with strong Supply Chain Management elements, Julian had followed Frank's recommendation to include CMU's Tepper, in Frank's hometown. Frank already had his Cape Spear Commercial gig lined up as a risk manager in the Canadian insurer's Pittsburgh regional office. Big league employers had lined up to pay Frank a bonus to skip business school as if he were a high school ace thinking of college baseball. It did not take a decade for him to form his own professional club, Frank Leonard Risk Consultants.

"It'll be fun," Frank had said. "You won't go to bars by yourself. I'll even buy while you stay broke."

That compelling argument had, eventually, had landed Julian on Leigh's dock with a slight hangover. He had since forgotten the truck and its driver had halos, too.

"Fate, aside, I deserve all the credit," Frank said.

"I felt sorry for him. I thought he had a broken arm or something."

Polly laughed. "Now you know he was thinking and walking at the same time."

"I had gum on my shoe, too."

"If it helps the story along," Frank added, "Julian survived on it for a week afterward."

"Really?" Leigh asked. "That's some gum."

"If nothing else," Polly said, "no couple will have the same origin story."

Leigh had insisted on supervising the loading of the sets she designed for a musical as part of her final theater course. The sets had to be moved from CMU to downtown's Public Theater for the performances. She had no business inside the trailer, but she had practically been raised in the warehouse where her father had worked. Particular about stowage, she felt the in-trailer positioning of the precious set's items was sloppy.

Cutting into Julian's comment, she said, "I know, I know."

"It looked wrong," Julian said.

"They would shift, banging into each other. I'd spent months on the set project. It was as close to a thesis as I'll ever get."

Julian had no business on the CMU loading dock that day. His part had concluded when he arranged the transport, as part of his Logistics and the Theater MBA course. As finicky about schedules as Leigh was about space, he wanted to be sure the one-stop delivery was on time. The ten-minute departure delay irked him enough to send him to the dock. He had not imagined an agile blond was the reason.

"See," Polly said, "there is a God."

"If there were, He would have delayed her take-off by two seconds," Julian objected, "it would have saved us a lot of time."

"God does not do sub-minutia."

"Besides, if you want to talk about expressions at our magic moment, I hoped she did not even see me. She looked royally pissed. Who's that beautiful when pissed? It was scary."

"Nice," Frank said.

"Admit it, Julian, you were too –"

"He's not all that shy, Polly," Leigh said.

"I was going to say *dumb*. He didn't think you'd be interested."

"For a while, I was right."

"Not really. I wondered what was wrong with him."

Frank leaned back in his chair. "Let me get this right: She was flying through the air as you stalked by."

"I didn't stalk."

"That came later," Polly volunteered.

"What?"

"Going to plays is not stalking," Julian said. "When you're in Supply Chain Management, you need some cultural enrichment."

"Which you needed so badly, you saw the plays twice."

"I concentrated on the excellent sets the first time through. Who knew there would be so much dialog and singing?"

Leigh had interned at the Public the following summer working on two plays. Julian went to those summer plays without a date. To the first – the one arranged by destiny – he had tried taking one of his more frequent dates, Vicky Dillard. He gave that up because Vicky summered in Vermont and because it went sideways when he saw Leigh changing the set during intermission.

"All right," Vicky said, cheerfully. "Who's she?"

"She?"

Vicky laughed at him. "The pretty, underfed blond moving furniture."

"Oh. I met her..." Julian lied, partway. "I arranged for the trucks to move the sets here. She had something to do with... loading them."

"Do I seem jealous? The girl moves furniture for a living?"

"Don't be a snob, Vicky," he joked. "One of us is studying to move all kinds of things for a living."

Vicky was in med school at the University of Pittsburgh. "While I'm off doing brain surgery in Boston, I'm sure you two will be very happy *moving* things in together."

Julian looked at Vicky, who looked right back. "I saw her once," he said. "For, like, a second."

"These things are like tumors." Vicky tapped Julian's temple. "They have to start somewhere."

"Vicky," Polly said, "was always smart. Prescient, even."

Leigh shrugged. She had never met Vicky.

"The future's not ours to see," Frank disagreed. "Doris Day."

"Qué?" Julian asked.

"You guys are too old for us," Polly said.

"No," Leigh said. "We need old souls for balance."

"You can't date them if you can't find them," Frank said, calmly.

Leigh laughed. "That sounds like a Match Dot Com ad pitch."

"He doesn't mean it that way, Leigh," Polly said. "Julian, either."

Frank and Julian glanced at each other but said nothing.

"What?" Leigh asked.

Polly patted her hand. "You haven't had the *talk* yet?"

"I'm obviously the novice." Leigh looked at Julian. "Look at me. What talk?"

Julian grimaced but complied. "you're an Irish Catholic Democrat and I'm an Independent."

"Yeah, and..."

"And we don't agree on every little thing."

Polly halfway snorted. "Somethings are big, other things are little. No offense, boys."

"Now," Frank said, "we are back on reasonable grounds, accuracy be damned."

"Ironic phrase, dear."

Leigh waved her hand in the air. "Conversational fourth wheel, here. It seems like I'm the flat."

"You're just slender," Polly said. "In a good way."

"Oh, thanks."

Julian contributed a kiss and "You're perfect."

"It's my only flaw."

Polly cleared her throat. "Okay. Enough ducking the big... issue." She turned full to Leigh. "The boys do not believe in the little things... like, souls. Or gods. Or Heaven."

Leigh's hand flew to her lips. "Oh." She stood up in one graceful motion.

"Wait," Julian said, horrified. He tried to stand, but Leigh stayed him with a hand on his shoulder.

Polly looked almost as stricken, Frank less so. He even smiled up at Leigh. "Polly's only flaw is that she's an agitator."

Leigh collapsed into her chair, laughing.

Polly joined her, while Julian's expression changed to one of confusion. Frank kept smiling.

Leigh gave Julian a reassuring kiss. "It'll be a few years," she said, "before I have to worry about missing you."

~ ~ ~

Frank and Polly were married first, on April 12, 1997, with Julian and Leigh standing for them. Shortly after the return from the honeymoon, planning for the latter's wedding began, with roles reversed. On September 20, 1997, a young, second cousin of Leigh's did the priestly duties for Julian and Leigh.

Her old pal, Mark Ryan had been waylaid on the way to ordination by multiple rule infractions, as everyone had expected.

The guest list was heavily weighted in favor of Leigh's Manning side. Julian had no family in town and few local friends that were not also Leigh's. He had very few work acquaintances as a rookie in his career. His family was spread all over the map, though his immediate family and several of his Dodd cousins flew in to fill in a few choice pews in the church.

From the very first, Leigh had warned Julian away from reacting to the religious aspects of visiting among the Manning flock. "Half of my grandparent's generation were nuns or priests. It may take another century for that to wear off. It is not your destiny to accelerate evolution," she said, crossing herself at the last word. "I'm serious. I can adore you all I want," she added, "and I will always remember you fondly."

Julian had grown up in a highly secular environment. His mother was a high school physics teacher, and his father was a purchasing agent for an aeronautics company. For Julian, God and Black Hole Emissions vied with Moon-based supply chains for a Mars mission as alternative research concepts with limited success. If he had not inherited his father's practicality, he absorbed plenty by age ten.

In sync on many things Leigh and Julian long left unresolved one big thing: The issue of *issue.* It nearly waylaid the wedding.

Simply put, Julian understood the utility of children as future purchasers and supporters of Social Security. That was as far as he could get. Leigh truly loved children, upon the condition that someone else would take them home. They were both career- and each other-oriented. Leigh also doubted her slim-hipped body as a *delivery system*, as she paraphrased Julian's lingo. "I can see rendering all kinds of things unto God, but I'm not rendering anything to Cesarean. You can write it down."

Julian reminded her of that line as they sat outside the office of a thirty-something pastor of their chosen Catholic church. The church and he were recommended by Leigh's elderly cousin who would perform the *I will* segment of the ceremony. The latter had already given his blessing, his eyes closed as an inside joke. They still needed the pastor's formal blessing paperwork and his agreement to co-preside at their wedding. One problem they faced: *The Church* pretty much demanded a commitment to do the necessary to have children right off the bat.

"Do not mention that we live together. I used my parent's address. Don't forget."

"We can still elope to Barbados," Julian said. "The trip is paid for."

"It's too late for that."

"Is he going to say we *have* to have *sex*?" I can live with that."

"No, he isn't."

"I mean, because I can agree body and soul with that. Halfway, at least."

"Not..." She whispered the next word. "*Fucking* now. Please."

"But he's going to ask, right? In so many Latin words."

Their relationship rested, in part, on the unexpectedly concrete footer that Leigh found Julian funny. He was testing her, at that moment.

"Yes. And you will nod sincerely if you can't manage an *Amen.*"

Julian feigned horror. "You want me to lie to a priest? In a church?"

"First of all, this is not a church. It is a *rectory*. Second, you're so anti-clerical, it would be hypocritical of you *not* to lie to the priest. So, tell me now that you will do it, or I will always remember you fondly."

"Two good points. Three, including the usual remembrance."

In the end, the priest put it, "Will you promise to perform the marital duties necessary to have children? That means no contraception, of course."

Julian hesitated but lied straight-faced, "Yes."

Leigh said, truthfully, "I love children, Father."

The young priest raised one eyebrow for each of them, shook his head and smiled.

Leigh breathed as they walked out the door. "Whew."

"Priest or no priest, he's pretty cool. He didn't believe a word I said."

The wedding forward as planned on a cloudless day and, Leigh's fear to the contrary, lightning did not strike. It did rain one day in Barbados, but that was fully explained by meteorologists.

Upon their return to Pittsburgh, Leigh and Julian concentrated on their jobs and each other. They progressed in their advertising and logistics careers to supervisory levels - resisting further promotions as *hands-on* types - and eventually bought not a house far from their small Shadyside apartment, in Quartermaster Township. Their place in the QM was not ten miles from Frank and Polly's house in adjacent Fox Chapel.

Their social life was limited to the occasional play at the Public Theater, monthly visits to Leigh's parents and weekend dinners with Frank and Polly. Frank and Julian met for *business* lunches once a week, with few exceptions. It seemed like plenty.

Julian was not a *kid kinda guy,* and Leigh was, at best, in no hurry, so they deferred the *Children* issue indefinitely.

Indefinitely turned definite in June of 2007, with Leigh's diagnosis of Ovarian Epithelial Cancer. The treatment was removal and chemo with a seventy-five percent chance of reaching the typical five-year horizon.

"That's as far as we go," said her surgeon even before the surgery. "Beyond that is a crap-shoot. No one can promise anything."

Leigh heard that as a promise of five years, at best. Julian heard five years and a roll of the dice.

It was in her to joke, "Who the hell counts time beyond the weekend, anyway?"

After one of those years consumed by agonizing chemotherapy and recovery, Leigh started counting. Julian, subconsciously, lost his concept of their time together.

"I love you Julian, but I'm not fucking doing this again."

"Whatever you want, I'll be with you."

The countdown hit a snag. By spring 2011, Leigh knew it was back, if not on her absent ovaries. In July, she chose a new approximation of Zero Hour.

She had Secondary Peritoneal Cancer and the only treatment comprised "washing" the inside of her abdominal wall with enough chemical to poison every surface to eke out a couple or, maybe, three more years. Leigh stuck with her plan and, ironically, her original timetable. With *no* treatment, she would *likely* make it through that fifth year.

When Leigh slipped by that count in July 2012, Julian became unduly optimistic. Leigh did not fool as easily but felt she had several months left, encouraging her to work on her last projects as diligently as her body allowed.

One of the projects involved the unexpectedly haunting dancing egg soft-boiled egg app for Julian, complete with a musical score. It worked almost well enough the one time they got to use it.

Chapter Four

July 2013

The egg app played *Top of the World,* by the Carpenters on the Galaxy tablet. Julian sat on his unmade bed and sang his side – presumably Richard Carpenter's – because he could not help himself. He would do it internally, anyway, though that would have sounded much better.

Julian could not sing. He could also not make the bed any longer. That was Leigh's deal. If water-boarded, he might have admitted to Frank and Polly that he was taunting her back.

If you want it made, come down here and do it yourself.

After several months and unopened gifts entitled, more or less, *Getting a Grip on Grief,* Julian finally had accepted that venting to the dead was an offshoot of watching *The Ghost Whisperer* with Leigh far too often.

He wore a plaid, cotton robe over his pajama set of a t-shirt and gym short. He owned lots of real pajamas – Christmas presents all – but they were formal marriage-garb. He pretended that he was saving them for his next marriage, not that the *comely* Erin – using as safe, neutral word to understate her appeal – or whoever, would go for him wearing Leigh's Christmas presents. She should have known that, the *she* who had insisted he *would* have a next wife.

"What about her?" Julian had asked, pointing to Jennifer Love Hewitt, the *Ghost Whisperer* herself. "She would come in handy, and you like her more than I do."

"For very different reasons. Sorry, Julian. She's a foot shorter than you. She'd kill your neck."

Julian had popped cervical disc trying to beat Leigh in tennis.

While advocating a *next* wife, Leigh had failed to approve a single, or married, actress.

Hey, how about...

Julian, at that moment, came up empty. He had not been to a movie or watched TV for months. He changed the topic.

You know about the pajamas, though. They'll have to go.

Julian liked to think he was *haunting* Leigh. He could not concede that he had gotten religion or gone all the way *off the edge* bonkers.

He glanced between the tablet and the cable box. 9:42, each said. He checked his watch, a Seiko beauty of a Christmas gift...

Damn it. I will have to ditch watch?

On the Galaxy, the Egg stopped moon-walking as the countdown clock neared zero and flexed its semi-realistic legs. Julian held the tablet up so he could see if there was any hitch between the Egg's time and that of the cable box.

No wonder I'm insane.

"... top of the...," Karen crooned.

The Egg was in the virtual air.

At "world," it settled its nether shell shallowly into the shooter, as Julian watched.

No. No hitch.

The music stopped.

"Ding! Oh, Julian!"

"I don't see the next wife putting up with you, either," Julian told the voice.

He had considered Leigh's insistence on his finding someone new – that she had found the right someone new in Erin Brennan – both morbid and unromantic, in *true love never dies* way. More lately, true, he had imagined some *next* scenarios, set mostly on Caribbean islands with two Pina Colada's, both for him.

I'm not supporting her bad habits. Not with your life insurance.

On the Galaxy screen, an announcement icon popped up with a Facebook Chat alert.

Julian pushed off the bed and trudged to his office. He liked the mood of the bedroom but realized it was time to communicate with the living.

As he passed the second bedroom, his tennis shoes caught his eye. He had a court reserved in a few hours and had gotten far as putting his sneakers at the foot of the bed. Digging into his closet for shorts had proven too... premature. It had become less so, but he had to get to the Chat. Jill hated waiting.

He spun his office chair to sit and clicked the desktop keyboard to open the chat window next to the Egg's stage. He muted the desktop's time app. As he expected, his cousin Jill Dodd was online. No one else initiated Chats with him, and she was long overdue to check for a pulse.

Leigh's laptop and the tablet kept mute pace with the desktop's app. As if he might find a variance, Julian triple-checked that the countdowns and the computer clocks matched.

On all three screens, the Egg hopped onto the glass and...

Something new happened: The timer app showed three “Ding! Oh, Julian!” exclamations in subtitles.

“Well, I'll be damned.”

The text disappeared as all three Eggs jumped down and used microphones to sing along with whatever song Julian was not hearing.

Julian clicked to the Chat window and saw Jill's.

***JIL** – Hi, Julian!!*

Jill was the most enthusiastic cousin he knew.

***JIL** – I'm sorry it's been so long.*

Julian typed, *At least I have something new today. The Voice sexted me.* His index finger hesitated over *Enter.* He stared at what he wrote: *Yes, I guess I think the voice is somewhat sexy, but, seriously, now, not in a* sexy *way.*

He erased the message and typed a less loaded response.

***JUL** – I am fine, Jill. I can't talk long. I have plans.*
***JIL** – Great!! Wait! It's not that Anna again.*
***JIL** – Leigh was not a fan.*

Polly had waited patiently for Julian to leave his house after dark. After six months, she insisted he come for dinner to their Fox Chapel house, ten miles away. He had gone there to dinner several more couple times without incident and their sons, deployed at Polly's mother's. The third time, Polly swapped out her sons for her divorced friend Anna. Polly warned Julian in advance, but he had assumed she was putting him on. Things had not gone too well, or too long, though he was vague in his recollection of it.

At the time, neither Frank, Polly nor Jill knew about the Erin Scenario. As far as Julian knew, Leigh had told no one about her preference, including Erin.

JUL – *No. Polly won't pair us up again. She likes Anna too much.*

JUL – *Besides, that was just dinner at friends, not a double date.*

JIL – *Uh huh. Tell Leigh that.*

JIL – *Did Anna's chair suddenly slide out from under her?*

JUL – *Yes.*

JIL – *You go, Leigh!!!*

Julian typed, *I was being a gentleman. Leigh is* but did not finish the second sentence. He had lapsed into present tense.

JIL – *Julian? Are you still there?*

He replaced the phrase. Jill was relentless enough about Leigh's being *present.*

JUL – *I was being a gentleman. We had finished dessert.*

JUL – *Leigh didn't do pratfalls.*

JIL – *Maybe, she's funnier now.*

JUL – *To me, it seems everyone is. Present company... and all that.*

JIL – *Present company, indeed.*

JIL – *You do know I'm not present, as in there.*

Jill was relentless.

Again, Julian did not finish his response, *Sorry, Cuz. One of us can't be pres,* annoyed with himself. It struck him that he had come to edit his all his interactions, even with those closest to him. With a sigh, he realized that meant only Jill, Polly, Frank and...

Oh, shit.

Julian edited his exit line.

JUL – Right. One of the present will soon be absent.
JUL –And it's just tennis. Bye.
JIL – Oh. Finally!! Footwork in the right direction!! Bye, bye.

Julian rested his chin on his left fist and mused that Jill's exclamation points looked like raining daggers. He closed the Chat window and watched the Egg on Leigh's laptop dance until the one-minute mark on the counters.

Something was off.

Julian turned Leigh's laptop until its Egg was directly facing him.

Facing, but not staring at him.

The damned thing was staring over his head. Julian had not noticed during the Chat, but these Eggs all had pupils stuck to the top of eye-whites. That was new and positively...

"Oh, for Christ's sake–"

Positively and intentionally *angelic.*

Suddenly furious with Leigh, he leaped from his chair, strode into the hall and slammed the office door. The result was very strange. He was looking at a closed office door. He had closed off all the Eggs behind a door. He had never done that.

There was no music.

There were no dancing eggs. No countdown.

Except, of course, there was the countdown, his countdown, in his head. He first shook his head and then began to nod off the seconds. He could not watch the door while he did it.

Julian let enough time run. He knew when to open the office door and when to step in front of his desk to see the ass-ends of the Eggs on all three screens hit their shooters.

Simultaneously, *Ding! Oh, Julian!* The text appeared on the screens and, internally, he replicated the voice. The timers seemed to hang in their reset.

For a fraction of a heartbeat, they, Julian included, were all in sync, but nothing happened. Julian had – but should not have had – the time to think.

Well, perhaps, it is always that way, and I just didn't notice. The hiatus doesn't matter. The three minute are all that matter.

For whatever interval, it was, the Eggs sat there, their eyes dead level, projecting out of the screens. Julian had half expected them to glare at him, but they did not. They had their usual vaguely contented expressions. The expressions, along with the limbs and improbable dance moves, had been endowed on them by Leigh, for him. The eyes were different.

The Eggs eyes were a message?

The illusion did not last beyond the next leaps off the shooters, but Julian would have bet ten dollars' worth of sanity that – despite their different angles – the Eggs' eyes did not see him at all.

They were focused *beyond* him.

~ ~ ~

Julian waited in the doorway of the second bedroom, listening to Linkin Park's *From the Inside*. Laying on the bed, were blurry Adidas tennis clothes, white shorts, and a contrasting blue polo shirt. The socks were white with a blue logo to match. He blinked the clothes into sharper focus.

Leigh had given him a reverse pair – matching blue with a white logo – as a semi-gag birthday gift. He had worn them out of the box for five minutes of Frank's delight but never outside the house.

"They are too precious to be worn," he had insisted when Leigh caught him burying them at the bottom of the crowded drawer.

"You are an adult, Julian. Your wife should dictate your taste, not Frank." It had been a good argument, if not a winning one.

After that, she had bought him colored socks for every color shirt or trim he owned.

He stood there, neither inside nor outside, wondering why Leigh had not found a song with *outside* in the title to balance Linkin Park.

Finally, he left the threshold and picked up one of the white socks. Lincoln Park's reign gave way to John Denver and *Annie's Song* after the inevitable *Ding! Oh, Julian!* Thinking of the inanimate, he put his right hand inside the sock. He was right-handed and could better manipulate the lips of the resulting sock-puppet.

After flexing its mouth and swiveling one-eighty, the Sock-Puppet said, "Three dimensions. Eat your flat, yellow heart out, Egg!"

Julian asked, "Haven't seen you for a while. What have you been up to?"

"Who is that?"

"Who do you think?"

"Oh, Julian. Hey. I've been laying low, but I've heard rumors. The Gold Toes? They never shut up."

"Of?"

"A spectral presence. What else have you been thinking about?"

"What have you seen?"

Sock Puppet shook itself and moved in on Julian's face. "Did you see *eyes* here, Mr. Observant?"

"I meant that in a metaphorical sense."

"Eyes are not metaphors to the damned Egg. It sees shit. Me, I see shit."

"The Egg was meant as a metaphor."

"The Egg was meant as a fucking meal, Julian!"

"That, too."

"And, ding, Julian. Get your ass dressed." The Sock Puppet waited a beat. "But be an adult and wear the blue socks."

Chapter Five

June 2012

Leigh pulled a Nike tennis dress from the second bedroom closet, which held Julian's clothes and those she had not worn for a while. She held it arm's length until her arm grew too tired to sustain the distance. It shocked her how quickly her arm gave out. She returned it to the closet. She could not bear to hold it up to her body.

What was left of it.

She then sifted through Julian's dozen Adidas polos, all gifts from her. Like her, Julian had needed multiple sizes. He had put on weight as she had lost it the first time around. The second time, he had lost some, at first, and, as home-bound as she, was packing it back on. She had to eat a little as often as she could, and Julian ate more as often.

"You shouldn't have to eat alone," was his tender excuse.

The tennis pieces had been handy, making minor gifts decisions less taxing. For whatever reason, Adidas fit him best and was easy to order online.

She had been all Nike.

How did such differently dressed people get along so well?

She selected a white polo with emerald green accents.

Irish green brings out the color of your *eyes, Julian.*

He insisted on contrast, so she grabbed the matching green shorts and lay the set carefully on the bed. He would have tossed them carelessly.

He would have been right, too, since the poly resisted whatever wrinkle thrown at it. She could not adapt at that late date.

It felt later every day.

Late enough that she needed to get his socks, the green ones. She smiled. He had a full array of color-matched ankle socks from Adidas and, if he rushed, he would certainly end up with blue.

She had gotten him that particular green outfit the previous Christmas, partly to encourage him to keep playing... without her.

Last Christmas.

God help her, she would be leaving Julian's sense of style to its own devices and Frank's influence. That was not a pretty picture, but it brought a smile.

Maybe, Erin will pick up the slack...

Her smile faded.

She wanted Julian to be happy again, more than anything.

Then what's with the envy?

Emerald Isle green! That's what did it. I can fix that!

Leigh went back to the closet and glumly switched the green outfit for the mid-blue.

How pathetic am I?

She turned toward the dresser, to exchange green socks for blue, her smile returning. It broadened when the solo angel caught her eye. The whole room, dresser included, had become Julian's preserve – or exile, as he called it – once the master closet filled with multiple sizes of suits, blouses, and dresses. The purses and shoes, thankfully, required no resizing.

Julian had resisted angels for years, but, ultimately, had caved on the lone interloper – her least favorite of eleven angels, cursed with severe eyes and lips pursed as if observing sin – but it had taken chemo to soften him. He had remained subversive, however, sighing whenever he opened a drawer after the last Eastern Orthodox Christmas Day. Each year, the angel stayed longer, until, after Last Christmas, it became a fixture.

Yes, Julian. I know it's over.

She did not want it to be over. Perhaps, the angels would help with that. Besides, she found them comforting.

Leigh took four small steps to the front of the dresser, one too many. She reached for the support of the dresser, but half of her ninety-four pounds transferred to the paper-mache angel. She felt a strange awe as the angel flew past her and landed on the carpet behind her left foot.

Sliding one hand down the face of the dresser, Leigh retrieved the angel. She slowly straightened and placed it on the dresser top. The left wing fluttered.

Oh, shit!

She could hear him: *They'll be much safer in the basement.* She would never see them again.

She manipulated the wing back into position and carefully returned the angel to its spot, as defined by a dust-free. Julian did not seem to notice dust.

I really need to buck up and use a feather duster. Feathers don't weigh anything.

Leigh steadied herself and opened the top drawer. Her spirits lifted as she sorted through the tennis socks to pick the blue ones. Largely for her benefit, she knew, Julian insisted that his ankles felt far better in the gift-worthy Adidas than plain Gold Toes. She shook her head at the thought, and the room swirled.

Before she knew it, Leigh was sitting on the edge of the bed, slipping fast. She pushed backward and closed her eyes to dam the next few tears. Instantly, she recognized that closing her eyes was a bad idea.

Crying was worse.

Julian will see.

As if beckoned, Julian called, "What time do I play, again?"

Leigh wiped her cheeks before feeling the coarseness of the socks near her eyes. *Oh, shit!*

She felt the socks with her free hand. They were noticeably damp. Even though Julian would never notice, she waved them as vigorously in the air as she could, which, she realized, was not very.

She cleared her throat. "You had plenty of time. Past tense."

"I've been busy," he said, with a slight echo courtesy of the close walls of the staircase.

Leigh leveraged herself into a standing position, socks ready to return to the drawer. Her knees buckled, and she felt lucky to resume sitting. She straightened her back.

Julian will see.

The thought kept running through her mind. She could not allow him to be any sadder than he was.

It was her fault, she knew. Aside from Frank and Polly, she had cut out all their acquaintances and all her family. She lacked the strength to continue to debate the merits of treatment. Anyone who could not accept her decision to forego chemo was too much aggravation for her. As a result, Julian bore the entire weight with her, with an unyielding spirit that was more valuable than he imagined.

Of course, he did not know what it was like, what she felt inside, physically and emotionally. It was crucial that she protected his innocence as much as possible, for her as much as for him.

It was very hard to do, but without him, everything would be much harder, maybe impossible.

Julian appeared in the doorway, holding a plate. Her stomach lurched at the sight of the sandwich.

"Are you sure you don't want to come with me?" he asked, stopping just inside the door. "Polly will be there, and we will stop at Renegade's after for a drink."

Leigh felt herself brighten and tamped down the enthusiasm. Renegade's was the one place she had been able to go. It helped that it was down the street from the Cancer Center.

Today, there was no chance.

"Erin is working today," he added, as an extra incentive.

She had not seen the girl since her last Center visit. Erin had started as their favorite waitress at Renegade's – their favorite hangout, when they still had one, and *the* stop after Cancer Center visits – to become another younger sister.

Uh... Step. Sister would be too wrong to be who's next.

"I'm tempted," she said. "But seeing you properly dressed is my limit, today."

"Ouch. We *have* been married... a great while."

"I meant coordinated."

"I'm not sure that's any better." He held out the plate. "This will help."

"Don't be offended, but *ugh*."

"It's my *Egg Surprise*!"

It took no strength at all for Leigh to look him in the eye, smile and say, "Julian Cochran overcooking an egg is not a surprise. Not in any of your parallel universes."

Julian puffed his chest. "The *culinary* name is Medallions of Vitellus Angelica. Voila!"

Leigh's stomach did a back flip when Julian lifted the bread. "I now officially hate Wikipedia."

He continued in a decent French accent. "See the pure white halos. On raw toast, avec creme de la–"

"It's Mayonnaise."

Julian pursed his lips, the word offending his French sensibilities. "Americans!"

Leigh kept her gaze locked on his, if only because the naked egg was nauseating. "You are such a whiz with just-in-time deliveries, and you can't count seconds up to one-hundred-eighty? How is that possible?"

He gave her his best abashed expression. "Seconds? That explains a *lot*."

"You are so good at playing clueless, that you have me convinced." She finally reached out for the plate. She looked at the plate and then at Julian. "I can try it. Maybe, the raw toast will help. For today." She put the plate on the bed. "You have to get the *soft*-boiled part of the boiled egg right. It may be all I can eat from here on out."

Julian dropped the facade, more stricken than he let on. "We're a ways from that aren't we?"

"Of course," Leigh lied. The *here on out* had been an unpardonable slip.

Maybe not. You have to prepare him.

"It's just that soft-boiled eggs are the easiest for me to eat that I actually like." She shrugged. "Dr. Morgan said we'd have a while yet."

"He said, to be exact, *X* months," Julian said. "We have yet to hit a month with an *X* in it."

"That explains the egg, too," she said. "There is no *X* in *three minutes*."

"Let me try again."

Leigh burst out laughing and coughed to end it. "For God's sake. Do not. Go make a mess of tennis, instead. I beg you."

"Are you sure?"

She was sure. "Have fun. That will make me feel better. That is your job, *from here on out*. Go."

"It is a shame tennis has no telecommuting," he said.

"If you don't get dressed, right now," Leigh said, holding out her hands, one with socks. "Tennis will need teleportation."

Julian pulled her gently to her feet. Neither of them broke the contact. Julian nodded toward the sandwich. "I have another recipe to use when I get back."

"No, no, please, don't do that," she said, holding on to him, waiting for her blood to rise, if only to her head.

It takes so long to get there!

"I can't handle anything more creative than Medallions of Vitellus." Leigh glanced at the plate. "Give me the damned thing."

Julian kept hold of her right hand and picked up the plate. He held it away from her. "You're sure you won't heave?"

"I can't promise you that." She pulled her other hand free. She took a bite of the sandwich and winced. "I'm going to enjoy purgatory if they have fries with it."

"You know you can always come back here for the Vitellus."

Leigh made a minor gagging sound and broke away. "Thanks. I can wait. You can't. Get dressed." She used the wall to help her into the hallway bathroom. Her goal was to flush the sandwich. But, then, she would feel bad for the toilet.

Still in the second bedroom, Julian noticed that the socks felt damp. He separated them and examined each, looking for signs of blood in the blue fibers. One sock was just a little wet. Leigh did not cry much when he was anywhere near.

He put the damp sock on his left hand and created a sock puppet.

"Like the Blue Man Group," the Sock Puppet whispered. "But with sound."

"How do you feel about soft-boiled eggs?"

The Sock Puppet made something of a face. "For us hard-boiled types, three minutes is too fucking short. If you know what I mean."

"I do, thanks," Julian whispered back. "But in the laundry for that mouth of yours."

Chapter Six

July 2013

Frank Leonard toweled himself off as he took a seat on the clubhouse level. He and Polly had finished a mixed doubles match, winning too quickly. He wore his mix of several brands, all navy-accented white. He was not a throwback to Rod Laver, but it was hot and sunny.

Frank was taller than Laver at five-foot eleven but three inches shorter than Julian. He was leaner, stronger and faster that Julian, even when younger and certainly at that late date. He tanned more easily. He did have less brown hair, but it had, again, the better, darker body.

In singles, Julian had never been a match for Frank. In mixed doubles, with Leigh adding to the height and speed, Frank and Polly had usually come up the short ones.

They had just finished a straight sets mixed match, allowing Frank the pleasure of watching Julian's tennis revival... from a safe distance.

He had tried to watch more closely over Julian in the months since Leigh's relapse. It had not been an easy task. Their friendship had started back at Brown and had remained firm ever since. Much as Leigh and Julian were homebodies, the four of them had gone out or stayed in for dinner twice or more a month. He and Julian had lunched once a week forever. Over the past ten years, Renegade's was the lunch spot of choice, even before Erin arrived there to pretty and spice up the place.

Once her cancer returned, Leigh and Julian had pulled back into themselves. Frank had coaxed Julian out to lunch every other week to keep his spirits up. A couple drinks, steak sandwiches, and Erin's banter had recharged Julian. After her death, Julian became more reclusive. Frank did not have Leigh pushing while he pulled. In the year since the two friends had gone to lunch a few times but never again at Renegade's.

The four of them had had such a good time together, spending so much time together, anniversaries, birthdays, tennis.

Birthdays. The gag gifts. Colored tennis socks Julian could not bring himself to wear...

Well, damn. That seals it.

Frank saw that the New Julian wore a pair of blue gift socks to match his shirt. Julian at least wore his white Adidas shorts. The tennis ball was lime green and went straight up from the racket. The next hit low on the net, the following bounced loudly off the far fence. Aside from the ill-fitting shirt and the equally saggy swing, Frank thought, this new Julian *looked* like a reasonable facsimile of the old Julian.

The once and former Julian was not oblivious enough to wear colored shirts, or socks, on sweltering summer days. As if someone above was watching – which Frank believed impossible – a small bank of clouds had appeared to protect current Julian from the effects of his poor choice. The sky had been clear until the moment his shoe touched the Har-Tru playing surface.

The old Julian had possessed a sweet top-spin forehand that had propelled tennis balls forward, well above the net and inside the back line. He had also shaved every day and got haircuts periodically. That Julian had, when on, had beaten Frank or, a few times, Leigh. In mixed doubles, the healthy couple had rarely lost to Frank and Polly or anyone else.

Another shot careened sideways. Julian looked up at Frank and shrugged.

Frank raised his thumb at another fence heard from.

Julian responded with a strategic digital substitution and a resigned smile.

Frank had known the current Julian appear gradually from a two-week husk over the previous eleven months. For those two weeks – right after Leigh died – an unrecognizable creature had arisen as a high-functioning zombie, with the attention span and job performance to match. He was lucky NorAm valued him so highly.

Frank was hardly surprised at the impact of Leigh's death, however, expected. Had he been inclined to do a risk assessment of Julian's chance at a steep decline – and that was Frank's expertise and his profession, after all – the result would have fallen between ninety-six and ninety-seven percent.

Frank saw the new version Frank whiff, again, had emerged as...

New Julian had not emerged at all, remaining wholly house-bound and unconcerned with his yard or beyond. He had taken a temporary and then permanent leave from his job, which he no longer needed and certainly could not do. Warehouses and retail shelves across the country would have been half full.

Or, like Julian, half empty.

As his second official act as best man, Frank had arranged for his father, Ben, to set up Leigh and Julian each with absurdly cheap forty-year, three million-dollar, universal life insurance policy. As Not-Emerging Julian's unofficial *financial adviser*, Frank had set up Internet auto-pay for all the bills, because Julian had developed a warped sense of personal time since 2007. Someone would haunt Frank if Julian's hot-line to the Cloud was interrupted due to non-payment.

Someone. Cloud indeed.

Frank had seen his old friend fret over average backhands. This one was merely bemused at being thrashed by a ball machine. It was a tough opponent for the current Julian, with barely one blue-socked foot on the comeback trail.

At least, he was finally trying.

Julian's lips moved the entire time, but not in disgust. His Moto phone played DJ'ed music and lyrics via a blue-tooth connection to the earpiece secured in his ear by an arc of plastic. Leigh's infamous app was in the Cloud, too. But for that presence, Frank and Polly may never have seen Leigh's bedeviled Egg.

They had not been inside Julian's house since three days after Leigh's funeral.

As far as Frank knew, no one had made it beyond his rare beers at the porch table since.

Julian tomahawked the next ball off his foot because he had glanced at his watch as the ball approached. Frank and Julian shook their heads in unison. Each was aware that Julian knew the amount of time and notes left in whatever song was playing on his phone.

The phone glowed through his back pocket.

Julian stopped, ignoring the next two shots completely. He laughed and resumed practice. Over the next minute, his returns rapidly improved.

"You need to get that song," Polly said, plopping her tennis bag next to Frank. Polly wore her uniform of white tight mid-thigh shorts and a white pin-striped polo that was intended to subdue her curves and failed. She shook out her long ponytail and handed him a bottled water and opened her own before she sat down. "It's like it changed him back to...." She dug into the bag and pulled out her iPhone. "To what he was, I mean." She began swiping.

"I'm guessing *We are the Champions.*"

"Why?"

"His play has always picked up for anthems. For a short song, that one's energizing as hell."

Polly showed Frank her phone. It displayed an array of small photos of attractive women, one a brunette with the name Anna Keller next to it. Polly touched it to give Anna the whole screen.

"I predict another mishit," Frank said.

"Anna is very–"

Julian whiffed as the machine's latest effort hit a divot and went sideways.

"Like that... swing was about Anna," Polly said.

Frank sighed. "Anna's Anna. Sort of an anti-Leigh–"

"Which was the point–"

"–but it was the whole idea that was off. Julian still prefers his time warp."

"So, I get to keep Anna?" Polly touched to return to her list of faces.

"Delete the whole Hot Prospect List," Frank said. "It hasn't been a year, yet."

"It's what Leigh wanted." Polly pouted as she scrolled. She scrolled all the way through her list, shrugging off one face after another until she reached Erin Brennan at the end. "When did you two last drink lunch at Renegade's? In Shadyside, for that matter." She showed Frank her iPhone screen.

Frank grin of approval quickly collapsed. "Wait." He took the phone and scrolled its screen. "You have Anna Keller first, and Erin Brennan last on that list? That's not my list?"

"Uh huh. Your list is not a list," Polly said, grabbing her phone back. She did not resent Frank's *crush* on Erin. He had had many, and they were as serious an orange soda. "Mine has multiple entries and is ranked by profession. Anna's an attorney."

"She's a lawyer."

Polly had manipulated the list a little, true, but that was her strength. Indeed, she seemed an oddity as a *stay at home mom* because she had so liked flipping customers. She found, however, that she needed more of her skill to manipulate one Frank and his two boys – *his* the operative word. "Erin is a *W*, waitress,"

"She's an *A*. She's an *attendant*. She is very attentive to me."

"Frank. Renegade's is a saloon, not a 737."

"They both serve me Jack Daniel's and a straw if I want it. Anna's always sipping *Pinot* something."

"Calm down."

"Wait. Isn't she an anthropologist?

"Not yet," Polly said, calmly. "Erin wouldn't belong on my list if she had her own endowed chair at Pitt's Grad School."

"Remember, you used endowed, not me."

Polly looked down her body, to make a point. If women were to let themselves go after having children, no one had forwarded that memo to Polly. "Her figure is certainly not an issue. She doesn't belong on my list, because these are suitable new *fish*, for Julian's *sea*."

"Good luck with that bunch of professional groupers."

"Let me ask this: Do you *want* Erin to be *Julian's* choice." Polly looked askance him. "Hmm. How would that work for you?"

Frank frowned. "It doesn't matter, Polly. Your fish menu is moot. Even Erin is moot."

"She is Leigh's first choice. Erin is smart, educated, funny, tall, borderline pretty–"

"She's all those things... and not the least *borderline*. But it's not about her." Frank acknowledged, to himself, that he was partly wrong. Julian had avoided their favorite lunch place in the post-Leigh era, specifically because of Erin. He was sure of that.

Julian can't face Leigh's choice.

Polly waited for him to voice what he was thinking. When he did not, she said, "Erin's young enough – and has those nice hips – for a few children, though why Leigh thinks Julian cares, I don't know."

Leigh. Is. Cares. English is not your second language, Pol!

Frank restrained himself. Polly had her own tense for Leigh, he had his. On the topic of children, they agreed, if not with Julian. "Julian had a hard-enough time sharing Leigh with Lily."

"Well–" Polly began before interjecting a sigh. "Maybe, that's less an issue, now."

"Not yet." Frank had to turn his attention to Julian, who avoided the back fence by sailing a shot over its tenth foot. "The inspiring anthem is over."

"So, why is it they're still running? The songs, the Egg?" Polly asked. "If she's not here?"

Frank and Julian had brought Leigh's laptop, complete with Egg Time, to one of their few 2013 lunches, none anywhere near Renegade's. Julian had quit trying to scam NorAm and himself a couple weeks before.

The conversation had been memorable.

~ ~ ~

Frank felt worried at the delayed work news, a little wounded, too. "I'm supposed to be your best friend and financial adviser. I find out today?"

Julian was barely *present.* "It was embarrassing."

"You don't need to work. Unless you're buying that island you've had your eye on."

"No," Julian said, hushed. "This did it." He handed Frank his phone with the app running, muted, on the screen.

"I saw it on your tablet. It's asinine. So, delete it."

"It downloaded to the phone."

"Just remove the damned thing, man. Come on," Frank said, exasperated. "You don't need it following you around. And, I mean, it has vodka in it." Frank didn't see the point of tasteless drinks. "Do you want me to–"

"Don't," Julian ordered, barely whispering. "That's not it. When I said *it downloaded,*" Julian explained, "I mean, it downloaded itself."

"She embedded it in your wifi network, so it would play on everything. Why she bothered is beyond me, but that's all there is to it." Frank handed the phone back.

He had no idea why, but the Egg disturbed him. That much had stuck with him from his first viewing. Leigh had gone to a heap of trouble to help Julian cook soft-boiled eggs for her. That was okay, but Julian's insistence on keeping an egg timer app, playing it constantly, month and month... It was hardly Leigh's legacy: Julian hated eggs, especially boiled ones.

"No." Julian looked so serious. "I was at work."

Frank's drink stopped in midair. He double-clutched before finishing it. "How did that happen? Was it an email?"

"No. It wasn't."

"Was it *pushed*?"

"No, I didn't have push enabled." Julian shrugged. "You see?"

"It's odd."

Julian gave Frank a look.

"Oh, shit. You didn't think–" Frank understood. "It was Leigh."

Julian was relieved that Frank got the point without Julian having to say it. "Pretty embarrassing when you say it, isn't it?"

"So, you quit?"

"Yeah. As in *get the message, already*."

"That was mine, first."

"I know," Julian said, with a smile. He got serious immediately, as evidenced by a lowering his voice. "But in the two weeks since, I haven't figured it out."

"Let me give it some thought."

"Please do. Do us both a favor?"

"But I won't tell Polly," Frank said, without more prompting. "You don't tell Jill."

"Oh, I haven't."

Frank closed his eyes for a second, deciding if he should ask the obvious question.

"Go on, Frank. Ask."

Frank signaled for another round. "Did you ask Leigh?"

Julian laughed. "How nuts do you think I am?"

"Pretty."

"Who else could I ask?"

~

Frank had, indeed, omitted the *spooky* download issue from his report to Polly. Some things had to remain between best friends. Possible madness was top of that particular list.

"You have to give her credit," Polly said, between sips of water. "She doesn't give up."

Frank hung his head and swallowed some familiar words.

She can't be fucking here!

"Even if he finally does," she added.

Frank looked up to see that that Julian was tipping one of many young, unofficial volunteers to fetch the dozens of tennis balls Julian surveyed. The kid would then use the rest of Julian's court time, as well as the machine.

Frank and Polly silently applauded the end of Julian's practice if not the performance.

Well, the machine was consistent.

Julian bowed graciously. He removed his smartphone and hit the screen. He removed the earpiece as picked up his bag off the ground by the net. He began his ascent to the Clubhouse level.

"Do not do that in front of Julian, Polly. Please." Frank knew Polly understood.

"Hm," she hummed, eyes skyward.

"Damn it, Polly."

"I didn't actually say anything.

"It's the same thing."

"Is it my fault that Leigh was so sure she could come back if she had to?" Polly asked. "And, as you can see, she had to."

"Finally, the past tense reaches present tense."

Julian arrived in time to hear Frank's words. "You either are speaking about Leigh..." He swung into a seat next to Frank. "Or you are diagramming sentences. Which no one has done since the dawn of email."

"Leigh," Polly said.

"Sentences," Frank said, just as quickly.

Julian laughed. "Okay. You were speaking in sentences with Leigh *present* in them."

For the next few seconds, all three exchanged smiles.

"In the sentences..." Frank spoke first. "Not next to us."

Julian stood up. "Yeah. Why do I feel the need of some vodka shooters?"

"How *appt*? With two P's," Polly summed up. "And so, *Leigh*."

"As afterlife evidence," Frank said. "That's not bad."

The three began walking to the parking lot, laughing before Polly stopped them both. "Frank. The song."

It was a rare occasion when Frank needed a moment to follow Polly's thought. "Oh, yeah. You perked up towards the end there. What was the song?"

"*We Are the Champions.* Queen," Julian said. "A perfect song. If you are playing for three minutes. Why?"

Polly shrugged. "Nothing."

"Nothing?" Frank objected. "I was right."

"Okay, okay," Polly conceded, with a devilish grin. "But I believe someone whispered that answer in your ear."

Chapter Seven

June 2012

Julian did not have to ask. He stopped the wheelchair well short of the huge wheelchair- and purse- friendly revolving door. Leigh lifted her luggage-sized purse barely off her lap before Dr. David Morgan reached down to relieve her of it.

Her post-relapse oncologist almost dropped it. "Good God, what's in here?"

"A tablet," she said, her voice raspy. "Which is funny, since I rarely use it. A bottle of water I rarely use. Obviously."

Julian took the bag from Dr. Morgan. "That's why I insisted on the wheelchair." He used his toe to lock first one side of the chair and then the other. "Leigh thinks walking is exercise."

"I need it," she said. She poked his mini-spare. "You need it more."

"You shouldn't have to–"

"Yes, I know. Love is measured in pounds."

"How British is that?"

"Veddy," said Dr. Morgan.

Leigh routinely protested the chair but on that day needed one, purse or no purse. She held out her hands on either side. Julian and Dr. Morgan eased her upright.

She liked the weightless feeling, so different from the usual. In a chair or in bed, she felt gravity had focused only on her. For the moment, she was free.

Once on her feet, the feeling dissipated. She held each hand tightly all the way through the door and out to the curb, where jogging valets dizzied her.

As two valets ran crossing routes around them, Julian said, "We need one of those..."

"Next time?" Dr. Morgan said. "Definitely."

"Nice try," she said. "Both of you."

Dr. Morgan wanted Leigh back. Chief of Abdominal Cancer at UPMC's Hillman Center, he believed in active treatment. He also believed the decision rested solely with the patient.

While Leigh had agreed to treatment five years earlier, she refused to consider it a second time. Her insurance covered as many visits and as many chemicals and photons as she could have wanted. Dr. Morgan had been straight with her. Any treatment would have brutalized her and gained her only a few years.

Six, zero and zero had been her choice. Dr. Morgan had implored her to consider treatment but only once. His first glance at Julian as he laid out options had told him the spouse was not going to help him.

"Look at me, Doctor," she had said, firmly.

"Don't waste your time," Julian had warned. "We agree. One hundred percent."

Her hand opened, but Dr. Morgan responded by firming his grip on her. He nodded leftward, in the direction of their car, and discretely revealed a pack of cigarettes in the white coat's pocket.

She laughed. "What's the name of that *Hippocritic* oath again?"

"Lungs are not my department," he whispered.

Once they reached a distant designated smoking area, they sat on one of its benches. Dr. Morgan lit up and sucked in deeply.

"Do you listen to yourself?" Leigh asked. "At all?"

"I listen to you," he replied. "The walk is great exercise. Next month, the perimeter will be up to a full mile. I'll end up outside to Renegade's."

"Where," Julian said, "our favorite waitress, will gladly serve you a butter-sizzled rib eye and a glass of sulfites to go with the cigarette."

Leigh suppressed a cough and then some. "I can hear you."

"I forgot you are sensitive to sulfites."

Dr. Morgan waited for Leigh to hit Julian, however weakly. It made him think of Lily, the inspiration he had never met. It reminded him, and he took his prescription pad from the pocket holding is cigarette pack. He put that off. "Speaking of Erin. Have you told her, yet?"

"I will. Today," Leigh said, glancing at the pad. "But she knows. Everybody knows. They know I won't change my mind."

"I will miss my favorite patient." Professional through and through, David Morgan still dreaded her appointments as they marked off the dwindling months.

"There are people you can help," she said evenly.

Dr. Morgan nodded and smoked some more. It was easier than talking.

"Doctor? David?"

He met her eyes. "Yes."

"I see...." She turned first to Julian, then, Dr. Morgan before she eyed his prescription pad. "I see you remember Lily."

David Morgan sighed out some smoke. "Of course." He took his pen from his breast pocket and began to write. He tore off one page and started on another.

Leigh and Julian watched silently.

He wrote a third and handed her all three.

Julian asked, "Did I mention my elbow hurts?"

Dr. Morgan gave Julian a professional once-over. "Erin told me you keep the Grey Goose in the freezer. Use that."

"Is it safe to use Leigh's medicine like that?"

"I meant the bottle." Dr. Morgan rose to grind out his cigarette out against the concrete waste stand. He sighed again. "One thing, please, Leigh."

"Yes."

"At some point, your lungs may take on fluid."

"Isn't that out of your area?" She smiled and stood up, taking Julian with her.

"Not in this case," he said, failing to match her expression. "If they do, come in, and we can drain it. We can make you more com–"

"We've talked about that." Leigh put her hand on his arm to stop him. She kissed him on the cheek. "Goodbye, David. My plan isn't right for everyone. It is for me."

"I'll be here," he said, well aware of the phases of her plan. "Good-bye." He held out his hand to Julian and repeated, "I'll be here. Even if you just need to talk."

Julian shook his hand. "Thanks, Doc."

Leigh took Julian's hand, and they walked toward their car.

Dr. Morgan knew about Lily. Dr. Morgan knew Leigh quietly suffered pain, depression, and anxiety. She would suffer more. That came with the territory. He felt fully justified in filling the Vicodin, the Valium, and the Ativan. He knew Julian used at least two pharmacies and no insurance to fill them.

He knew the hyper-vigilant DEA would take a dim view of the high doses. He knew he did not care.

He understood that she was stockpiling.

She had briefed him on what *Lily* meant.

He had a sense of character. Julian was an incurable optimist. Leigh was simply incurable and had resigned herself to her fate; however, deep down, she was still a daily optimist.

The time was in days, at that point.

He judged it at better than fifty-fifty that she would wait too long to use her stockpile. She would be too weak, too sick.

It would, then, fall to Julian, the guy with a lousy sense of time.

David Morgan watched them walk to their car, removing and lighting another cigarette by reflex.

He feared that Julian would insist on seeing what the next day would bring when there would be no next day.

It will be all about time, *Julian. Don't fuck it up.*

~ ~ ~

Julian pulled the car as close to Renegade's as possible, leaving room for the door. He waited for Leigh to relieve her purse of its two pint water bottles and a wallet half as thick as it once was. Then, he jumped out. He circled the trunk and got to her before she made her third attempt to get out.

He need not have bothered banging his knee on a fender. Leigh had decided to await his hand. As she struggled to her feet, she thought about how she loved his hand and how easily it used to lift her.

She spotted a car leaving a nearby space and guided his eyes with hers. "Go. I'll be fine."

Julian just smiled back. It was such a hopeful smile, heartening and sad at once.

He'll be fine.

And I want him to be. Well, almost *fine.* Good *is good.*

She would be fine, too, getting as far as a table. Leigh knew how to conserve energy. She also knew that she was feeble when first standing. She looped her purse around her forearm and used the cars parked on either side of her for support. She waited beside the cars until she felt some strength burn down her legs.

As bad as her weakness was, it had been worse under chemo. She knew what to expect and how to deal with it.

Her next goal was the sturdy handle on Renegade's front door. She made that and checked on Julian.

He had lost the parking space to another car. She was sure he had laid off his horn for her benefit, and it had cost him the precious space. Renegade's had no lot of its own and relied on meager metered parking. Most of its patrons walked to it, and a few of them wobbled home after 2:00 AM.

Renegade's had a two door, or *airlock scheme* – to use Julian's phrase – that Leigh used to the max. The two doors kept cold air where it was supposed to be. The encased foyer had a narrow bench. Leigh avoided the sitting, standing up being the worse problem. Through the glass of the inner door, she spied to an open booth.

Julian missed the space, I can't lose my end.

She took a deep breath, pulled on the heavy inner door and strode to the booth, claiming it with a toss of her purse onto the vinyl seat. For thirty seconds, she stood leaning on the booth divider. She scanned the restaurant for Erin.

Leigh had always been comfortable in Renegade's interior, even after treatments. It had a beautiful, old-style bar rail on one long wall and a parallel line of booths on the other. Two rows of sturdy wood four-tops sat in the middle. For years, she had admired the perfect spacing of everything, far more than the details. She savored the look.

It might be the last time I'll see it.

She spotted Erin at the far end of the bar, loading a tray with drinks. She waved.

Erin smiled back and gestured with the tray that she would be a few minutes.

Leigh nodded, and Leigh slid into the booth with a less than graceful motion. She opened her purse and took out her tablet. She knew Julian would be a while parking in a distant lot. That gave her time for the tablet and brainstorming. Erin was part of that.

She had known Erin Brennan for five years, tough years. Providence had placed Erin at Renegade's just after Leigh's original diagnosis. The girl had the empathy to read the Cochran's expressions when they entered, and she wore her heart on her T-shirt sleeve. Of course, she had already met Julian a few times at lunch, and it took Leigh only a few visits to know how Erin felt about her oblivious husband.

Erin looked more Irish that Leigh. She had large hazel eyes, with more green than Julian's and expressive to a fault. Her natural rust-brown hair was long enough to pull into a short, tight ponytail for work, but not to her shoulders. When down, it framed her soft, elongated oval of a face perfectly. Either look suited Erin's fair but often blushed complexion, which benefited from being less delicate or light as Leigh's.

She had a faint spray of freckles highlighting the subdued cheekbones on either side of her slightly upturned nose. Perhaps more than anything else, Leigh envied Erin's well-defined, naturally rosy lips.

The lips aside, Erin enviably filled out the latest Renegade's uniform. After a decade of miscues involving tights, bare legs, short shorts, mini-skirts, tight, scoop-necked T-shirts – Renegade's had settled on its best look ever, especially for Erin: An extra-long, Renegade-crimson oxford-style shirt, belted in black with dark gray skinny jeans. It flattered legs and her waist-to-hips curve. From Erin's earliest Renegades outfits, Leigh knew Erin had the legs Leigh had always wanted, long, nicely solid and a little shapely in the jeans.

Though only an inch plus taller than Leigh's five foot seven inches, Erin occupied the eye more than Leigh ever had. Where Leigh was the definition of *slender*, Erin possessed the shoulders, breasts, hips, a defined waist and legs Leigh never had. Though not as voluptuous as Polly, Erin made Leigh feel bony.

Well...

Leigh had seen the *type* Julian dated. Privately, Frank had described Julian's type when Leigh asked the question after a few months dating Julian. Tactfully, Frank admitted she was not it, but he told her not to worry. He repeated what Julian had told him in response to Frank's own question of the subject of Leigh's suitability.

"Type?" Julian had responded when she mentioned it. "Oh, that old thing? I have a new one."

None of them had met Erin at that point, but she fit Frank's description of Julian's *old* type, in a *T* or not.

Leigh sighed and turned her attention to another type of type, one that was certainly not Julian's. If nothing else, he disliked eggs in any form. She did most of her work on her laptop, but it had become too heavy for her to carry. She liked to tinker to take her mind off of the dismay and discomfort of appointments.

She removed the stylus and toggled to her graphics app. Graphics was not her strength, but she had five stop-action pages of her Egg figure, with its stick legs in progressive positions. She planned to replace the sticks with more realistic legs, and she knew whose legs would be the inspiration.

All Egg versions had standard *smiley* expressions. On the last page, only a text box displayed, with the phrase *+ 3 Min Songs.* She returned to page four, highlighted the Egg and copied it. After pasting the image onto page five, she added the new legs and erased the former sticks, but only on that page.

Still not quite Erin's legs. Getting close to what I remember.

Skinny jeans would be too obvious.

She flipped back to page four and took a deep breath, the kind she avoided when Julian was around. She feared he would hear the gurgling she felt.

She blurted a gallows laugh.

He'll just think I'm hungry.

And he'd be right, under the nausea.

The hunger-nausea combination tormented her. Without eating, she would remain weak, but the thought of food made eating a chore. She had been hungry all day. Julian had not helped matters with his rib-eye comment, but she would have loved to eat one. As long as she didn't have to see it or think about it, she could eat two, medium bloody.

On cue, Julian entered, saw Leigh and hurried into the booth. "God damn. I hate parking here."

"I think we covered that exercise is good for you."

"I run the stairs at home. Besides, Dr. Morgan frowns on hypertension." He held out his hand. "May as well give me the scripts. I'll run them in on the way home."

As she dug into her purse with one hand, she tapped the table with the other. "I can map pharmacies for you." She lay the three prescriptions on the tablet.

"That's okay," he said before dropping to a whisper. "Walgreen's is..." He did a double take at the screen-view under the scripts. "Oh, shit."

While his eyes were occupied, Leigh raised an eyebrow for Erin.

Erin had surreptitiously approached the table from behind Julian. She put a finger to her lips. At Leigh's expression, Erin stopped and waited. Her heart clenched so hard she could feel it. If they were at Renegade's, they had been at the Cancer Center.

She loved them both, Leigh as an older sister; Julian... There was very little she could do about that.

Oblivious, Julian spun the tablet around. "You need to work on your ovals," he said, with a feigned scowl. "This is not your best work."

"Because it is not an oval."

"And who shot it in the tush with arrows."

"I gave it real legs on the next page," Leigh lied, aware of the irony. Erin's perfect thighs were not two feet from Julian's shoulder. "It's for a timer. And it talks."

Julian rubbed his forehead. He knew where the conversation was going. "Saying?"

Leigh lowered her voice and added some Erin-style huskiness to it. "Count to three, buster. Or else."

He nodded. "Sorry, but that voice is hard-boiled. All the way."

Erin cringed. Their egg-cooking debate predated Leigh's relapse, but it had taken on serious overtones since Julian had taken on the cooking chores.

"Oh, Erin," Leigh said, suddenly. "Hi. I didn't see you. Sit with us, for a minute. If you can."

Erin sat down next to Julian. It had always been easy to be playful with Frank and, therefore, Julian. To call them her favorite male customers – and she had a lot – would be a silly understatement.

Frank and Julian had eaten and drunk lunch once a week at various places, Renegade's the most frequent from their days in surrounding Shadyside. After their first time at her table, she tried to schedule her lunch shifts on their usual day of the week. Within three few months, Renegade's became *the* spot for their lunches. When Julian brought in Leigh, Erin's feelings became horribly jumbled. She could not pretend she believed Julian was single, but the darling Leigh put her in a funk for weeks.

Erin used a well-shaped hip to move Julian over. When he moved, she followed. "Who, in God's holy name, needs a hard-boiled egg timer?"

"Nobody," Leigh said. "Nobody who counts."

"Oh."

Julian edged toward the wall. "Never do a job halfway."

"And, *ah hem*, how do you like your rib-eye, Mr. Cochran?" Erin asked, not willing to push her luck or her hip. She stayed put.

Leigh displayed faux shock. "His what?"

"That was supposed to be our secret," Julian said. "By the way, how much of a tip should I toss you for a salad?"

"Sorry," Erin said. "Mr. Touchy."

"Whose hip did the actual *touching*?"

Leigh watched the exchange with more interest than ever before. She felt a detachment that was not unusual anymore.

Not out of body. *Yet.*

It feels comforting.

She enjoyed their rhythm. The sparkle in Erin's eyes was sweet. It felt oddly satisfying, the sensual young girl engaged with her husband, side by side – and across a distance from Leigh – occupying their shared space nicely.

They do *fit, don't they?*

"Hey," Erin said. "You made room for it."

"Erin," Leigh said. "That didn't sound like a complaint. If I had hips, they'd be jealous."

Erin's eyes shot to Leigh's, betraying how fretful she felt for going as far as she did. She recovered quickly. She popped out of the booth and slid in next to Leigh, hip to hip. "Better?"

"I wasn't hitting on you, young lady," Leigh said. "Just making a point."

"Oh. Still."

"Uh. No. But we can still be friends."

Erin wrinkled her nose. "Ow. That really sounds lame when someone else says it."

"If I can un-join you two," Julian interjected, "I'd like to have my, uh, *usual* order. A chef's salad. Give Leigh the eggs."

"We haven't had chef salad's since I've been here," Erin said. "So that would be your *unusual* order. We have the usual romaine salad with shallots, pancetta, Tuscan olive oil with balsamic vinegar and eggs harder than even you can cook."

"Pancetta?" Julian asked. "That must be new."

"Yes. This decade."

"Do you still serve American beers, *young lady*?"

"To you? Only when Frank's not here."

Leigh had never cared before, but she yielded to an impulse to pin down Erin's age. "I hate to admit it after five years, but I don't even know just how young you are."

"Leigh, you can't ask Erin that."

"How *young* is completely proper.

"Yes, it's even a compliment," Erin said. "I'm twenty-six."

Leigh nodded. "That's about right." She had thought out-loud. "My guess, I mean."

"Me, too," Julian said, taken aback. Erin had seemed at least that age when she had first waited on him, and Frank.

Often, Erin felt she was getting too old too fast. Seeing Julian's response, she felt ghastly young. "I will be twenty-seven in September."

"You had just graduated," Leigh said. "When we met you here. You were looking for a teaching job."

"Still am," Erin said, embarrassed. Julian and Leigh were professionals. She was a life-long Renegade's waitress. "You know that special one. The one that doesn't require me to be all hard-boiled and carry a chalk and a taser."

"How do we keep returning to that topic?" Julian asked. "I thought only Leigh was obsessed with talking eggs."

"And dancing," Leigh added.

"Oh, crap."

"To what, Leigh?"

Leigh looked from Erin to Julian. "Every last three-minute song I can find."

"Oh, crap."

Erin laughed. "I love that idea. You know it's the perfect song length?"

Julian dropped his head. "Here it comes."

"Yes, I do. And I do not believe in coincidences."

"Is it a coincidence you both know that perfect song trivia?"

Leigh and Erin turned at the same moment to look at each other. Their eyes locked for as long as a vibe took to rattle them both. They looked at Julian.

"That's not the sign I meant," Leigh said. "Erin and I are just both well informed. It's about the *three minutes* you can't count."

Erin slid out of the booth. "If this were a Prime-Time soap, we'd find out we were twin clones or something worse. Over tea. They always drink tea, now, for some reason. What happened to coffee?" She stopped babbling.

"Tea sounds good. Clones, not so much." Leigh laughed, but she sensed that their relationship had changed. "And soup, for me."

"Give me that Romaine salad, hold the eggs," Julian said. "What is the soup?"

Backing away, Erin said, "Egg-drop."

"It's a sign," Julian said, "for me to fast. But I will resist."

"I do worry. For a sensitive man, you are blind to even the most obvious *signs*," Leigh said, her hand on Julian's. "As for Erin, around you, she can't help herself. You are an easy target."

"She seems to do just fine, thank you very much."

Yes, Julian, she does.

"It's actually minestrone."

"I think I can handle that," Leigh said, feeling optimistic.

~ ~ ~

As it turned out, the minestrone did not work out for Leigh. While Julian ate his salad, she sketched on her tablet. Her most recent embellishment, wings on the Egg, did not work, either. She erased them.

"How is this app of yours going to work?"

"I don't know for sure, yet. It doesn't have to be in a browser to run, but that looks like the easiest way to go. We use Chrome for our browsers. The tablet, I'm not worried about for now, but it runs Chrome, too. But I've never done an app or gadget before, so, at this point, I'm guessing."

"I'd wish you good luck," Julian said. "But I don't."

"I'm not relying on good luck these days," she said. "Hence, the need for an egg-timing app. With music, you can hear from upstairs. I don't trust you to take the tablet to the kitchen."

"Three minutes isn't very long," Julian said. "Are there any songs that short these days?"

"I already have some," she said. "Most are old. Good, but not recent."

As was often the case, a wave of fatigue swept over Leigh, all the way to her face. The outing had been fun and enlightening, but she had to leave. "Julian."

Julian waved to Erin for the check. He dug out his wallet and removed his American Express.

Erin grimaced and rushed over with the bill and handed it to Julian. She nodded toward Leigh's soup. "Let me take that off for you." She grabbed the tab while still in Julian's hand. For a beat, she held both. Then she blushed and opened her hand. The check fluttered to the table. "The soup, I mean. You can keep those."

Julian was examining his fingers. "We're lucky. Paper can cut deep."

"Oh, God. I'm sorry–"

"He's kidding."

Erin blushed again before she picked up the check. "I should get that by now."

"Yes, you should," Leigh said with a smile. "It's not the soup, Erin. It's me. It smelled so good, but, as usual, these days, I could use one less of my six senses."

Erin sighed. She needed them to stay a little longer, even three minutes. She might never see Leigh again. "Let me knock the soup off. I'll be right back."

Leigh watched her go. "Do you have cash?"

"Sure." He opened the wallet again and exchanged the card for cash.

"I want to pay cash," she said. "I want to give Erin a big tip, and I want her to have it all."

"Okay." Julian started to count the cash.

Leigh put her hand on the bills. "I'll do it. You get the car. I can't walk far."

Julian studied Leigh. "Okay. I can take a hint." He got out of the booth but waited for Erin to return. "I'm off to get the car. Would you walk Leigh out when you see me?"

"Of course." Avoiding any awkward pause, Erin hugged Julian, hard. "Bye."

He had been planning a quip on the tip but thought better of it. "Thanks, Erin. Leigh, wait for Erin."

"I will."

Julian added an "Okay," and headed outside.

Leigh and Erin watched until he reached the door. Erin kept watching, but Leigh shifted her focus to Erin, whose eyes began to tear when the door closed.

"Sorry." She could not look at Leigh.

"Don't be. Sit down."

Erin perched on the end of the booth's seat until she finished wiping her eyes with the napkin. When she realized it was Julian's she started tearing all over again. "Damn it. I didn't want... It was the last time. The last appointment."

"Yes, it was."

"I'm not going to see you again, am I?"

Leigh had to keep Erin focused. "We'll see."

Erin looked surprised. "Really?"

"You have that louse of a boyfriend, right?"

"Sometimes. Donny. He's not much..." She did not want to say what she was thinking, what she was always thinking, comparing Donny to her standard. It would hurt Leigh. "We're tepid." She knew immediately that Leigh had read her mind.

"Don't settle, Erin. Not with your heart," Leigh said, emphasizing each word. "You can afford to wait."

"Okay," Erin said. She added a sly smile. "Poor Donny."

"Don't ditch Danny tonight. He had that animation program?" Leigh asked. "You sent me that Obama caricature doing the hula in the grass skirt."

"I did?" Erin flushed. "Oh, great. That's embarrassing."

"Julian thought it was hilarious. It was well done. Can I get a copy? Of the program?"

Erin perked up. "Sure. Donny never puts anything away. I mean that isn't beer or pizza."

"I want to finish my timer app as soon as possible," Leigh explained. "Decent animation will make it less annoying for Julian, but I'm too slow at it. I don't want..." She stopped, realizing she had to lighten her tone. She laughed. "I don't want to starve to death before my time. Literally, soft-boiled eggs will be all I can eat. I definitely do not have time to train Julian to pay attention to the clock. It's not in him."

"Oh, God."

"And, yes, you need to know that I am still nixing the chemo. As in period. amen. I hope you understand."

"You know I do."

"I can't go through that again. Not for more uncertainty."

Erin bit her lip.

"Don't do that," Leigh said. "You have pretty lips. And no, I'm not hitting on you, again."

Erin laughed. It was such a gift, Leigh's laughter. She pulled herself together enough to ask what had been on her mind for months. "Do you need my help. With the... *Lily*?"

"Oh, no. Not with that." Leigh did not want to subject Erin to that conversation. "That animation program, though. I'd love that."

"It will be nice to know I can help," Erin said. "I would do anything for you."

Leigh took a deep breath. Her voice had lost an octave. "There is one more thing." She held Erin hostage with her eyes, but then let up. In that instant, she decided to defer the talk with Erin about what she needed for Julian. "Please bring me the animation program, to the house, as soon as you get. There may be something else I'll need to ask you to do. Don't worry, it is nothing dire."

"Name it, Leigh. Name it."

At that moment, the car appeared in Renegade's front large window. "It's Julian," Leigh said, mostly to plant a critical seed.... in very fertile ground.

"Julian?"

"Yes. Outside. The car."

"Oh. Oh, God. Of course."

Leigh began to slide out of the booth but needed Erin's help. "I wish I could do it on my own. It's been a long day, and I've been sitting too long."

Erin helped Leigh to her feet. It scared her to feel Leigh's weakness as they started for the door. As they went, though, Leigh steadied and grew stronger.

"That's better," Leigh said. By the time they passed the outer, door, Leigh released Erin's hand. "Let me walk alone from here. I am shaky, so stay beside me. Being an invalid is not part of the plan. Not a total invalid."

"I'll call you tomorrow. About the program."

"Don't tell Julian." Leigh stopped at the car and blocked the passenger door. "At this point, what he doesn't know is good for both of us." She stepped back to open the door, kissed Erin on the cheek and got in the car.

Julian waved, and Erin shut the door.

It was not final.

She would see Leigh again. She could put off the dread a little. She was pleased, too, that Leigh believed that she could help in a small way.

Leigh believed in her, believed she was intended for something better than Donny.

Don't settle, Erin.

Wow.

Erin stood watching the car drive away. She knew she was transparent to Leigh, who was so smart, so aware. If anything, Leigh was more attuned since her making her decisions.

Leigh knew Erin's heart.
You can afford to wait...
Oh, God.
Leigh meant Julian.

Chapter Eight

August 2013

On the desktop, an Adobe Photoshop window, five times the diminished Egg timer window, displayed an enlarged photo of Leigh and Lily. The Egg danced in half of the screen on Leigh's laptop, far off to the right. Julian needed the full range of his mouse for Photoshopping. A newly framed print-out of Leigh and Lily sat atop the dark tablet to the left of the desktop monitor.

The largest of the photos were four x six, some older ones were smaller. Julian scaled them up to eight by ten, the size of the frames he had ordered from Amazon. He also increased the pixel count. He had done just that for the on-screen photo of Leigh on a Caribbean beach somewhere. It was one of the nicest he had come across. The rare light sunburn brought out some fetching freckles on her fair skin that appeared in no other photos he had processed.

He assumed it was early in their marriage because Leigh's face had a more rounded look. As she grew older, the proportions of her face changed to a more oval shape. It had been so gradual, neither of them noticed until looking at old island photos when planning their 2002 vacation.

Try as he might, he could not place the beach any more accurately than a million square miles.

As an extension of selecting Leigh funeral photos, he had undertaken the long-term task of scanning all their photos.

They had never been shutterbugs, so the task was physically and electronically easy.

He had known from the start that he would be unable to annotate the scans. He would like to remember that uniquely *freckled* beach. He printed the photo and loaded one of the hundreds with Leigh holding Lily.

Two Lily-Leigh shots, along with two of Leigh alone – Julian vetoed any including him – had made it to Leigh's memorial service. As she had arranged, everything was handled by Ryan & Sons Funeral Home, down the street from her girlhood home. Julian vaguely remembered wondering if she would have approved of the placement of the four photos.

On the day after Leigh's death, Polly suggested the idea of converting snapshots of Leigh into framed photos to display at Ryan's. Leigh had previously bound old friend Deake Ryan to a closed casket and Julian, even in his state, had not wavered. The photos would have to do.

"The photos were her idea," Polly said, at the time. "She just told me."

Frank raised an eyebrow. Julian responded with unfocused eyes.

"No, *before*. Jeez. Lighten up, Frank." Knowing her words would elude Julian, she added, "It's too early for that."

Polly then tasked Frank with the purchase of a Photoshop suitable ink-jet printer – Julian's three-year-old lacked suitable resolution – within twenty-four hours. Polly guided Julian's selection of favorite photos. Scanning and printing were mechanical enough for Julian to handle.

Julian's memory of the process was mostly anecdotes from Polly, though he recalled a firm *no* or two.

Once he realized how little he had contributed to the photo selection, Julian dedicated himself to a brute force archive project: He would scan every photo he had. He had plenty of evenings to fill.

He outlined the photo from above Lily up. "More Leigh, less Lily for the current crop," he said, cropping the lower third of the shot. "No offense, Lily. Yes, I agree. You are very photogenic. But don't be a *phot-hog*."

It was too bad Polly had not found the photo for the funeral. It would definitely have made the cut.

The photo was unusually nice shot of one of Leigh's look. Leigh was an imperfect subject of Julian's limited photographic skill. Her complexion and frame of light blond hair tended to wash out in most lighting. More to the point, none of his snapshots truly captured her.

That beach shot came as close as he ever had. It was destined for the living room coffee table.

As he cropped the photo to zoom in on her, he wished he had half her eye for layout. She would have picked the perfect proportions without conscious thought.

He did his best and scaled the cropped image back to eight by ten. At the high-quality setting, it printed slowly. Julian watched the Egg dance on the desktop and laptop screens until *Ding! Oh, Julian* appeared, and the Eggs sat, however briefly.

He then switched placed a Christmas four by six onto the platen of the Cannon and returned his focus to the Desktop's shrunken app window. Resisting all of five seconds, he unmuted.

What are we playing now?

He glanced left toward his watch as if the watch would challenge the accuracy of computer time. He reflected on how computers, tablets, and cell phones had driven watches over the retail cliff. His was a good one and kept up.

Dance to the Music, by Sly and the Family Stone, played infectiously. The Egg had something in its Micky Mouse mitt.

Julian glanced over at the larger window on Leigh's laptop for confirmation of the new addition.

Sure enough, the Egg flashed a fancy smartphone, complete with headset and wired connection. It was also doing a weird Texas Two-Step to pre-funk, acid-soul and Julian smiled at the mismatch. Leigh had been a fan of almost all dancing, including, improbably, Julian's.

"Keep it fresh. Nice work."

He blew up the window size to full screen in hopes of determining the brand of the smartphone. In her commercial sets and her ad campaigns, Leigh had included subliminal, *brand-emphasis* details. He was not disappointed. The phone was a Samsung, very similar to his own. She had given it a tiny, readable time display that perfectly matched that of the laptop.

"Wow. You are unreal."

He returned his eyes to the desktop and enlarged the app. Same Samsung...

The time was off.

He checked his watch and then his own Samsung phone. Both matched the desktop.

The laptop was off.

The difference so startled him that it took him a dance step or two to see what was the stunner. He checked his watch and phone again, then the desktop and the laptop. There was no doubt.

Leigh's laptop lagged the desktop by exactly three minutes.

No fucking way!

He wanted to laugh, but the attempt failed.

Three minutes.

Julian believed in coincidences more than fate. Certainly, flukes on computers were common enough. Julian shoved his mouse off its pad and butted Leigh's laptop against his desktop.

He closed both the Egg Timer windows and reopened them. The time remained off. He zoomed in on both tiny Egg phones. Their times were off by three minutes. Too amazed to be angry, he closed the app on the laptop and navigated to its Time Reset Routine. He enlarged that window to full screen and manually reset the time to match the desktop display. He glared at the hundredths of seconds flick away on Leigh's laptop with the corrected time.

Satisfied that the change had taken hold, he closed the time-reset window. He put his index finger on the touch-pad, ready to trigger the Father Time icon. He did not get that far. His eye caught–

What the fuck?

The lower right taskbar time display was, once again, three minutes behind.

Julian opened the time-reset routine again. The displayed time was back to the three-minute error.

As if being extra deliberate would matter, Julian carefully reset the time and did it again. Before he closed the time-reset window, the task bar displays the corrected time. As soon as he closed the window, the taskbar dropped three minutes.

He was fed up with squinting at the both computers tiny taskbar time display.

In the desktop, he entered the Windows time routine window, he first clicked on the third tab that allowed him to choose one of several resizable clock dials for the laptop's screen. Its time would represent the taskbar display, using digitally rendered hands. The one he picked had a colorful, modern flair – proudly claiming a *gradient of Caribbean colors between aqua and turquoise* – with dark *crimson* bars for hour markers. The exact time was shown in the companion digital display below, using the same colors. The digital display extended to hundredths of a second. He turned off the taskbar time display.

Fuck you.

He positioned the clock face at the extreme right corner. He sized it so that the clock dial was two inches in diameter, making it and its adjacent digital read-out much easier to read than the taskbar version.

Without a microscope.

The second tab presented options allowing a manual setting or syncing with Microsoft's and others' online clocks Julian opted to sync the laptop with the Microsoft version. It worked perfectly. The right corner dial and digital displays matched.

He closed the window.

Satisfied with his desktop work, Julian duplicated the process on the Laptop. The new corner analog dial and its digital clock showed the correct time, exactly matching the desktop.

Julian closed the time-set window.

Both the clock face and the digital display fell back three minutes faster than he could see it happen.

He quickly reentered the time-set routine and reactivated the laptop's taskbar display. It read slow by the three minutes. He turned if off again with a vengeance.

Julian observed – as if from a distance – the laptop's new, stubborn clock face. It was both easier to see and harder to avoid.

"Damn it, Leigh."

He shut down her laptop, closed its lid and flipped it over. Forcing his breathing to steady, he waited until the *Ding! Oh, Julian!* appeared on the desktop. He removed the laptop battery. Normally, he would have counted off twenty seconds to restore the batter.

This isn't normally.

He waited to the next *Ding!* On the desktop to snap the battery in place. He rebooted Leigh's laptop.

It took less than another *Ding!* for the Window's logo to clear and the normal screen to appear. Egg's Father Time icon took its time to appear. He hesitated, even closed his eyes, before he glanced at the clock face and glared at its digital counterpart.

Gone!

He could not resist restoring the taskbar time display. It was the same. He turned if off.

If those three minutes are gone, I'm not going blind looking for them.

He breathed. It seemed foreign to breath. He turned off the desktop. He took off his watch and put it the desk drawer. He did not want to see the time, right or wrong.

He used both hands to close Leigh's laptop, to steady them. He pushed them against Leigh's laptop to rise from his chair. He glared at Leigh's laptop.

"Try Dancin' in the Goddamned Dark, Dumpty."

Julian picked up the framed photo and studied it.

"You just look like an angel. Right?"

Julian turned his back on Leigh's laptop and left the room with the photo. Time, Leigh bedeviling him or not, would have to straighten itself out. She would have to take her place among the other local angels.

It was all he could handle.

~ ~ ~

The angel invasion began as an infiltration. For their very first Christmas tree, Leigh imported from home, a six-inch gilded cardboard angel for the tree top. It was the most basic of angels in the firmament. It had a shirt board cone under its thin cloth skirt. The upper body was painted lightweight plaster, sporting two wings. Wired above its sweet round face hung a ring of a halo. As a girl, her family had long used such a spartan angel.

When they ambled through stores around the holidays, Leigh admired display angels. Julian should have been suspicious, but it seemed harmless window shopping. She had dozens of presents to buy for parents, siblings and favorite cousins. He bought just for her, with very specific guidance.

One Summer, a Christmas store opened on the road to a winter vacation spot in the Laurel Highlands, a couple hours' drive from home. *Christmas All Year Round*, it called itself, subtitled, *It's July Somewhere*. Headed for an anniversary weekend in the mountains, Leigh insisted they stopped to see what could sell in an unusually sweltering September. The shop was very air-conditioned. If not frosty enough to see a breath, it created a dramatic difference in climate. There, Leigh saw her first elaborate angles and bought a foot-tall version to replace her childhood one.

"Early retirement. Does she get a golden parachute?"

"I thought you were sentimental."

"I may never see one this nice again," she said.

"So, you push our present one into early retirement. Does she get a golden parachute?"

"She will get an emeritus position. I'm thinking mantle."

"She'll look lost."

That comment caused Leigh to buy two for the mantle, keeping the tree-top angel for the tree top.

The shop remained open for too many angels to count. It became a cool Summer weekend break destination. Even Julian had to admit the angels were works of art. Before long, a foot-tall tree-topping angel required a shorter tree. Every taller angel usurped the prime spots on the mantle with others spilling onto tables and into other rooms. Leigh went so far as to make one herself for the porch, though she had been in a dismal mood when she did. Its expression fell into the non-comforting category.

Julian once again surveyed the living room population. The angels usual post-January, cardboard homes lay empty in the corner of the room. He had intended to move angels to a box after what they knew would be her last Christmas, but he had kept putting it off. Leigh had felt comfort in their company, so the boxes descended to the cellar, empty.

A month after her death, he brought up the boxes, but the angels pushed the boxes back to the basement without much effort. After a barely noticeable Christmas, he tried again. He did not derive any comfort from them.

They annoyed the hell out of him.

Julian had been more successful in printing the photos of Leigh but limited the display at any one time to six around the house. He rotated new ones into the mix from time to time. He had several folders full of them.

He hoisted the beach photo he had just printed and framed and replaced the one centered on the coffee table. It did not look quite right. He wanted to show it off more.

"Where are you when I need you."

She could just see how it was supposed to fit.

He tried it on the mantle between the two mantle angels. He stood back and tried to *Leigh* the room. It was off. The angels were too dominant.

They'd fit *in the boxes just fine.*

"Okay. You with the wings," he said aloud. "You've had a year to commit. Tomorrow it's either the clouds or the cardboard. Your choice. I need the room."

From their impassive faces, he assumed tomorrow would be another day of barren heavens and boxes.

Leigh's photo went back to the coffee table. He planned to do better by it later, mostly by banishing a few angels.

Julian put the former coffee table photo on the third step and walked through the dining room to the kitchen. He opened the freezer and studied the cache of Grey Goose Vodka. Perhaps, he thought, Grey Goose would help him channel Leigh's spatial gift as he dealt with the living room.

There's not that much Grey Goose.

Maybe, tomorrow morning while the angels are asleep.

No, that's vampires, damn it.

He closed the freezer door and walked to the bottom of the stairs. He picked up the photo and walked up to his office. He opened Leigh's laptop, glared at its blank screen and sat down heavily. He retrieved his watch and put it back on. He did not look at the time. He hit the power button his desktop and let it boot.

He opened the laptop, and it began its resurrection from sleep mode.

He had thought that.

Resurrection.

That's zombies. Maybe, Vampires, too.

While the laptop awakened, he removed the back from the picture frame and freed the photo. He added it to the latest, and fifth, file folder of her photos.

The desktop screen displayed its time window. He opened the timer program and listened from the middle of Bon Jovi's *Everyday*, lowering the volume. The laptop screen sprung to life. Julian stared at it, then at the desktop screen's clock. The laptop's clock display was three minutes short of the desktop. Julian double checked it against his watch. It agreed with the desktop.

The laptop timer program played the same song and showed the same dance, perfectly synced to the desktop.

Except for the three minutes!

He checked the tablet and then his phone. Both were synced perfectly to the desktop, but with the desktop's time.

Only Leigh's personal laptop had lost the three minutes.

Julian felt lightheaded and took a deep breath. He opened the file manager, Windows Explorer, on both machines and navigated to the programs directory. He studied the subdirectories for some hint of the Egg timer program, a "timer" folder, a Java folder, an app folder. He found nothing.

"Where did she hide you?"

He opened a utility program that listed all the services on the laptop. He duplicated the listing on the desktop. Several services and programs had vague or meaningless names. He closed each one. None affected the timer program, not even the ones that closed the web browser and Windows Desktop and Windows Explorer.

The screens were blank except for the timer program. No time was displayed. He still could terminate the running timer programs, and he did so.

He brought up the services utility again, but the list showed nothing useful.

He rebooted both the desktop and the laptop. The wait seemed interminable. Perhaps, he considered, he had lost all sense of time, and Leigh's laptop was letting him know.

Leigh.

Time doesn't matter, Leigh!

"Don't lie to yourself, pal."

The computers came up with their dueling clocks ticking three minutes apart.

Julian grabbed the laptop and leaped up leaving the chair spinning. He ran the short distance to the master bedroom and looked at the cable box. It always had the right time.

"I mean it's Comcast."

He checked the cable box against his watch. It matched.

He dreaded the next step, but it was the point of his sudden exercise. The laptop dissented.

He turned on the fifty-five inch LCD. He checked three different weather channels. They all matched the cable box. The laptop kept pace.

Behind by three minutes.

However disconcerted Julian may have been up to that point, he was stupefied. He sat on the bed and breathed again, realizing that he had stopped. When he felt up to it, he went back to the office and set the laptop on the desk. He spun the chair and sat down.

I have just begun!

Matching the laptop routines with the desktop, he moved the cursors to the time read-outs on the task bars and left clicked. The set-time routines opened. The so-called long time showed the computers to be three minutes apart to the hundredth of a second. Both were set to automatically sync to Microsoft's internet time function.

He changed the laptop's setting to manual and entered the correct time. The laptop took the change and was in sync with the desktop, to within a tenth of a second or two.

Julian watched the time click by, for a minute, two, three, four, all perfectly in sync.

"Gotcha!"

He closed the time-set routine.

The laptop clock flicked back three minutes.

Laptop... what? Eleven, Julian, zero.

While all this back and forth, triumph and failure had been going on, the timer program had ploughed on. It was playing *Build Me Up Buttercup*, by the Foundations. Julian liked the song – and most of Leigh's playlist – the first hundred times he had heard it.

Go ahead, for God's sake!

Break his *fucking heart and be done with it*!

Julian went to the Web again on the laptop. He googled *time set programs* and found a five-star version, *NTP*

WristWatch. He liked the retro name and downloaded the program's *exe*, an executable install file. He installed the program, a step he has done hundreds of times over the years. Not as often as he had heard *Build Me Up, Buttercup*, mind, put plenty of items. The program created a suitable *wristwatch* icon on the laptop's desktop, more like his sleek Seiko than a Rolex.

The final step of the install was the message: *Run NTP WristWatch.*

When installing programs, Julian had never hesitated. For once, he did, three times. He felt the edge of a very bottomless pit beneath his finger.

Julian got up from the chair. He stretched. He paced the hallway. He looked down the dreary, narrow staircase. Turning, back to the staircase, he balanced precariously on the top step.

He had no idea what he was testing. He did not think, he just did.

Backflip?

His field of view narrowed to the table in the alcove, its photo of Leigh and the angel next to it.

"Okay," he told them. "Let's stop doing this."

He stepped firmly forward with his right foot. His left foot slipped, but his balance was well forward, and he stabilized himself halfway to the angel near the window. He lifted one foot and then the other.

"One of you is ambivalent."

Julian resolved to take down the laptop's clock. He returned to his desk and *WristWatch's* waiting message.

He hit the *run* icon and watched as the *WristWatch* ran, its window overlapping the timer window. A new song, Neil Diamond's *Cracklin' Rosie*, had started, along with a new dance routine. The timer window popped over the *WristWatch* window, vying for his attention.

Julian moved the two windows cleanly apart, like two squabbling patrons at a bar.

"Play nice."

Despite the implications, Julian vocalized, often. Leigh, Lilly, angels, photos, televisions, Comcast, computers were targets. He did it a lot to himself, too. He did not recall doing so with such frequency until – it had taken a while for him to diagnose – five or six months after Leigh died. Maybe it was around Christmas.

In the end, he spent most of his neurosis addressing...

You know who you are.

"Ready if you are."

The *WristWatch* window did not talk back, but it waited, stuck on the laptop's lag. Windows had had its chance, through various options, automatic, manual, daylight savings, time zone, 24-hour format. Windows had a variety of internet time services, Microsoft, a few Network Time Protocol standards – that's what NTP stood for – and US Navy for the automatic feature. Julian had tried Microsoft and somehow felt US Navy was his last-ditch option. He was not there, yet, so he chose the first NTP.

The time immediately changed to the correct time in the *WristWatch* app and on the laptop's clock. Julian did not celebrate, and he despised the tickle of hope he felt. He closed the *WristWatch* window and waited.

In a blink of his eye, three minutes disappeared, yet again.

I wanted it to be wrong?

Have I gone off the cliff after all?

Julian rejected both ideas. He hit the watch icon and reopened the app. He tried the manual set, with exactly the same result.

With a triumph of will, Julian arrested his fist before it displaced half the keys on the laptop.

"Leigh abhors violence. But I warn you, she just punched that ticket."

He punished the laptop with a glare, instead.

"Take this!"

He hit the power key and, sanely, addressed only the faintly whining laptop.

"No orderly shutdown for you. Tomorrow, I go nuclear. Actually, I'll have the Navy do it. Think it over. Carefully."

He popped up the power off routine for the desktop, yielding options.

"I'm done with of options."

Still, he picked *Sleep*.

Julian picked up the tablet and tucked it under his arm. He turned off the office light and made his intention clear.

"Remember. Tomorrow, laptop. Last fucking chance."

Chapter Nine

July 2012

The cab pulled up in front of Ryan & Sons Funeral Home. Leigh gave the driver a forty percent tip because, she thought, she would not be tipping a lot in the future. She opened the car door and tried to stand.

Not the best idea.

She went to her Contacts and hit Deacon Ryan. His photo appeared as the phone dialed.

"Is this the proprietor of Ryan and *Son* Funeral home?"

"Very funny. You called me. And I know my contact has my picture. And you asked that two sons be here today."

Leigh had known Deake, Mark, and all the Ryans from about age two. Deake was her age, Mark a few years older. She never played together after a very young age, because the boys were too rough, too daring with the skinny girl's life. It was a wonder the more wicked of the two, Mark, had gone into – or had finally been allowed into – the priesthood They did play soccer and, later, baseball and some basketball. Leigh relied on her sense of *position* as well as speed and finesse, none Ryan traits.

That was then.

"I'm outside. I need a strong Irish arm, or I'll sit here all day."

"We've got four."

She did not expect Father Mark to get to her before she hung up. Deake lagged by thirty seconds. Taking Mark's hand to get up, she said, "You must really need the business."

"We are downsizing, lass."

"We'd be happy to wait in, your case," Deake said, pleasantly. He took her other arm. "Dad's friends are still supporting two pubs down the way, if in a less tipsy way." Deake and Mark used brogues when they thought it would be more amusing. The closest either had gotten to Ireland was their last shot of Jameson, ten minutes before, as Leigh could detect.

Though one support would do, Leigh allowed both men to escort her into the funeral home. They led her to the main sitting area. She was pleased that Deake had left the furnishings as she had suggested for the renovation a few years earlier.

Deake had already set out all the materials for discussion. She had made arrangements for funerals before and knew the direction she wanted to... *go*.

Seated between Deake and Father Mark, she opened the top Casket catalog first. She flipped through several pages to find the first one marked with a yellow PostIt note. "I still like this one."

"That's what I wrote up for you."

"You're sure I can rent it?"

Raised as a boy just two floors above the casket showroom. Deake Ryan had a darker sense of humor than Leigh on her darkest day so far, but he kept it tamed. "Absolutely. Dry cleaning is included."

"That's efficient."

She pulled out her checkbook and began writing.

"Whoa!" Deake objected. "You don't pay now. I'll bill you later..."

Leigh looked at him.

"Not that much later."

She resumed writing the check. "I don't want to lose it to a better offer."

"Oh, my sainted mother. Wait. Knock off the dry cleaning, since I'll hop right into it myself. I'll need it once Julian finds out I let you do the planning and paying by your lonesome."

"I'm not alone. Besides, I want you to hold the checks. I'll bring Julian in later – not that much later – and pay then. You can tear up the checks. If something goes wrong and I can't, you won't have to bother him."

"For a sweet thing, you are devious."

"Thank you. Besides, you know Julian and priests. No offense Mark," she said, patting the priest's knee. "And thanks for coming."

Though not as close as the three were, Julian and the brothers had gotten along well in their few encounters over the years, usually at funerals or weddings of the extended Manning clan.

"I can't say I'm happy to help," Mark said. "And I do agree with Deacon."

"That's new."

"Julian will put him in that casket and nail it shut with Deake's teeth."

Leigh did a double take and laughed. She looked at Deake "That would be fun, Deake. You and I can come back together. I'm not sure Julian will believe just me. You, without teeth? He'll believe that."

Deake crossed himself and looked at Mark. "Well? Is it feasible?"

Father Mark said nothing but did smile.

"Uh, Mark," Deake said. "Your answer is being recorded for quality assurance."

"Playing along is not lying, Mark."

Your teeth may not be strong enough," he told Deake. To Leigh, he said, "Julian is a hard nut. He is shy on faith... especially in anything, Deake would have to say, alive or toothless."

"True, on both counts."

"Thanks for the guidance, Father," Deake said. "Let's move on from the pleasantries."

Leigh took a look at the second proposal, for the funeral expenses. "Good. I'll write a check for this, too..." Leigh leafed through the pages of the second book – the urn book, also with Post-its but of various colors – and stopped. "I want to lock in that special price you mentioned."

Deake chortled. "It's not like you're getting a discount from the usual discount."

"Oh, really. We baked mud pies together."

Deake looked around her at his brother. "I don't recall that. Do you?"

"We weren't much for baking."

"Oh, that's right. You left them in the sun at my house." She punched Deake on the upper arm. "I got a lecture on cleanliness and Godliness thanks to you two."

"Even at a young age, I was ordained to be ordained."

Leigh broke out laughing. When she stopped, her tone turned serious. "Mark, I'd like to pay for the crypt, today." She lightened up. "I want to guarantee my reservation."

"It's not necessary, Leigh," Mark said. "It's half empty. And, no," he added, "we are not recruiting."

"I want just it done. Off my mind."

"I know. Yes, you can."

Deacon asked, "Oh, Leigh. Who balances your checking account these days?"

She made a face. This is from my Fidelity account. Julian won't see it for a while." She turned to Mark. "I need enough space for two, you know."

"Does Julian know about *that* plan?"

"Yes. I've told him that *clichés will keep us together*." She added a lilt to the last.

"Uh huh," Deake said. "And Julian probably said, 'I'll have to *urn* it.'" His impression of Julian was quite good.

"He hasn't," she said. "But I'm sure he will." She turned one more page in the Urn book, then used a PostIt to go to her previous selection. "It's not like I'll change my mind." The Urn was coated in deep blue ceramic and had an angel on opposing sides. She looked at it for a moment. "It's so well balanced. I will let Julian can pick his own. It will probably have little trucks on the sides. Once they are sealed in, no one will have to see how awful they look together."

Deake pretended to brighten up. "Special orders are much more expensive."

"That will be Julian's problem." She turned to another PostIt and began to remove it. "Are these all marked for me?"

"No, only the blue ones. The ones with angels on them." Deake shrugged.

"Anyone I know?"

"No. They are from the Polish Ward. Walt Kowalewski retired last year."

"You're kidding. Ryan's with Polish customers. To think I lived to see it."

Deake held her eyes as he said, "This is so fucked."

"Great, Deacon," Mark objected. "I'll be needing a new sermon now."

When they stopped laughing, Leigh turned to Mark. Can you still drive me...?"

"Of course."

She waited until they had her arms and stood with them. Her knees wobbled. She sighed. "I'll need you about half the way."

They nodded and tightened their grips.

"Oh, Mark. Could we stop by Renegade's? I have to pick up something from Erin.

"Ah, Erin Brennan," he said as they began to walk to the door. "Deake, who last saw the inside of a church, Erin or Julian? Present company excepted, Leigh."

"Thanks."

"A toss up with those two. They'd have to find one first" Deake said, using a medium brogue.

Leigh looked at Deake. "They would, wouldn't they?"

~ ~ ~

The quiet mid-afternoons gave Renegade's staff plenty of free time to prepare for Happy Hour and dinner. Leigh refused to take the first empty booth, testing herself. She tested out only to the first seat of the second booth. She did prefer the first side, even when healthy. She liked watching the activity of the place.

Father Mark made sure she had settled herself before sliding onto the opposite bench.

As usual, the odors of the place nauseated Leigh, initially. She waited for her stomach to acclimate.

Erin returned from a kitchen run and waved to Leigh. Once she dropped off her order, she hurried over to the booth and reached in to hug Leigh. She then kissed the man with her on the cheek. She said, "Hi, guys–" She stopped when she realized the man was not Julian. "Oh shit."

Mark narrowed his eyes, playfully. "A cheery hello is more standard."

"I mean, holy cow. Father Mark. Wow." Erin wrinkled her nose and looked at Leigh. "Good for you. This guy is a major upgrade."

"Nice of you to remember me, young lady," Mark said in his most fatherly voice.

"About that–"

Leigh rescued Erin. "Mark's driving me home, Erin. I think I can manage some tea, today."

"I think I will succumb," Mark said, "and have a draft of the blessed Guinness. Does someone else have to serve it?"

"Okay, I get it," Erin said. To Leigh, she added, "I'm glad you made it. I'm out of here in a few minutes. I'll be back." She disappeared into the office area of the restaurant.

"You should not torture her."

"She promised me she would come to mass last Palm Sunday. How hard is that?"

"Ask Julian," Leigh said. "He dropped me off." She gestured toward the bar. "Who is more surrounded by bad influences? Erin or me?"

"Another toss up."

"Don't use the word *toss*, right now, Mark?" Leigh grimaced.

Erin returned with a small, Renegade gift bag, a tea and a half glass of Guinness. "That's the sacramental size, Father."

"You are so going to Hell." Leigh's hand shook enough to create waves in the tea, so she put the cup down.

The others pretended not to notice.

"We priests are not allowed to give up," Mark said, drinking half the stout in one swallow. "Which is why I keep coming here."

"Uh huh." Erin handed Leigh the bag. "I told you I'd be happy to drive it out, today. You know, the program."

Leigh nodded. "I know, but I was going to be with M... Father Mark." She smiled at Mark. "Kind of clearing the way."

"Okay. I would have been happy..." Erin sighed. "The USB is in the bag."

Leigh removed the drive from the bag and looked at it as if the thing revealed its contents at a glance. "I'm really excited. I know it's silly, but it is my last..." She felt bad that Erin cringed.

Mark did not react.

He was such a pro.

"It's just a chance to finish a project again," Leigh lied. "I miss that about work."

"Something I should know about?" Mark asked.

"No," Leigh began, before she changed modes. "Maybe. It is a device intended to torture... uh... *guide* Julian until your boss can deal with him, mercifully I hope."

Mark looked at Erin. "Do you have one for me? Our tools are limited, ever since the Inquisition ended. Too soon for Julian or the souls of some others." He arched an eyebrow her way.

Erin favored Mark with an exaggerated gulp, "Would it count if I drove a *sainted one* home for you?"

"Can I go, too?" Leigh asked.

"It might. I don't make those decisions."

"That would be great, Erin. You and I could use some girl time. No offense Mark."

"If I took offense, I'd have to forgive you *after* I finished my Guinness. We all have our priorities."

Yes, we do.

"Mine's the rent money."

Leigh and Mark watched as Erin hurry away. When they faced each other again, Mark said, "What is it? About priorities?"

"Oh, I just struck off a few with you and Deake, today." She looked away. "The day's not over, yet."

"I won't ask."

"You might not approve, so I wouldn't answer if you did."

His eyes clouded over. He put his hand on hers. "I won't ask because I can't dispute the answer."

She patted his hand. "It's not that. No, but today *is* still important."

~ ~ ~

Thankfully, Erin had lots of chat to contribute on the drive. Leigh had only to comment occasionally. She understood that Erin had correctly assessed Leigh's frail state and intentionally carried the load. Erin was not like that, normally, being more into Julian-style banter. The empathy – and the reflex to act upon what she sensed – strengthened Leigh's view of Erin's character.

And, yes, her soul.

Erin took a breath. "So. Father Mark, huh?"

"It surprises you? He used to have a crush on me."

"Really? Oh, tell me more. I need some dirt on the guy."

"Well, there was some of that," Leigh said. "I think I was four."

"I'll bet he had a crush on you longer than that."

"Could be." She sighed. "Today was just some spiritual planning... Actually, it wasn't. It was practical."

"Yeah?"

"Yeah. I want to make sure I don't end up... on your mantle."

Erin's voice rose a full octave. "No. No. Don't say that!"

"You don't have a mantle, do you?"

Their laughter banished the tension. "No. No mantle. How do you feel about a dresser?"

"In a sexy girl's bedroom?" Leigh asked. She kept the tone light, but she did not like the thought at all. "I don't think so."

"Uh..."

"I know, it's not like I could see."

"No, I meant..." Erin looked over. "You think I'm sexy?" She hesitated. "Really? Like slutty? I think that's the Renegade look."

"Like wholesome."

"Oh, thanks! I *will* end up alone." Erin's laugh was forced. "I need a tattoo or something."

"Please don't," Leigh said, a bit too earnestly. "Although, I think Frank would like you in tattoos."

"Great." Erin took the bait. "Would Julian?"

"I've never heard him say, tattoo and Erin in a sentence, if that helps. Erin, I've heard plenty, tattoo, never."

"Enough about real art," Erin said, after a beat. "I should brief you on creating the virtual kind?"

"Ah. Can I make a two-dimensional dancing urn?"

"Leigh!" Erin cried. "That's so... *bad*."

"I won't, Erin. I promise only to use it for good."

"Okay. I'll hold you to that. I'm serious." Erin reconsidered the threat. "How, exactly, would I enforce that?"

"I think we touched on one way. The dresser option?"

"That would be so sick and morbid coming from anyone else." Erin shuddered off the feeling. "Okay. The program. Number one: It is easy. It has a library of stock animations that someone augmented without permission. You can download lots more for a small fee. Two, it will run on your Tablet or your phone, as well as your computers. You can design it as an app or for browsers. It uses HTML5 for video, not Flash, which is on its way out, from what I'm told."

"I'll use whatever takes less time. I don't have a lot."

"Do you talk this way in front of Julian?" Erin kept her eyes on the road.

"Of course, I do. He is not at all sensitive about time."

"Oh, God," Erin said, with a laugh. "You're scaring me."

"You know how he is. He's wonderfully sweet, but he is so optimistic, he misses a lot." She hesitated. "Most of the time, I thank God for that. On the other hand, I need a dancing egg with a sledgehammer."

They drove in silence for the first time. Finally, Erin said, "The program can make a whole bag of hammers boogie. So, it should work."

"Thank your boyfriend for me, too."

Erin stiffened. "Well..."

"Uh oh."

"Danny doesn't exactly know I borrowed it."

"Really."

Erin said nothing. She wrinkled her nose.

"Erin."

"I borrowed it when I packed his things." She threw her hands off the wheel for an instant. "Okay."

"Oh, Erin, I'm sorry."

"He never..." Erin stole a glance at Leigh. She rolled her eyes, comically. "A girl has to have standards. You know?"

Leigh knew exactly who she meant. "They should be quite high, in your case."

"Hardly." She shrugged. "I just got a tip from a really good friend."

"Better now than later. That's how I feel."

Erin swallowed and hesitated some more. "I could have hung on a little longer. Danny was so bad, I mean." She looked at the Cochran house as she turned into the driveway. "I just couldn't." She turned off the car and just sat for a second. "Besides, the relationship wasn't really fair to him."

Leigh took a few breaths, preparing to get out. "You are sensitive as well as wholesome."

"That is so excellent."

"Will you help me up the steps to the porch?"

Erin almost jumped out of the car and circle to the passenger door. "God, I'm sorry. I got wrapped up in myself."

"I wanted you to. It was fun to hear you talk about yourself. I know you. I mean I really do know you, but like to hear details." With the aid of Erin's hand, Leigh stood up and moved away from the door "Would you close that for me? Just to be on the safe side. I'm really not that weak. It's just my balance is shot when I stand. Like it metastasized to my middle ear."

Erin gave Leigh her arm and asked, "How do you do that? Joke about it?"

"Humor is a form of night vision goggles–"

"Okay. Now, wait," Erin said. "Night vision goggles?"

"Do you think I'm past learning?" They started up the stone stairs to the porch. "Admittedly, only from TV?"

"Sure, but not night vision goggles."

"Not right now, but later, when you get a chance, think about it."

When they reached the top of the stairs, they walked slowly to the bistro table, and Leigh sat down. "Those stairs seemed like such a good idea... at the time."

Swinging into the chair opposite Leigh, Erin asked, in a hushed tone, as if volume excused the question. "Can I ask you something, Leigh? Why wasn't Julian with you?"

"You do know what I was doing with Mark? Father Mark?" Leigh cocked her head.

"I can guess."

"After years of those so-called business lunches, you know Julian pretty well."

"Mostly, Frank does the talking," she said quickly. "And the flirting."

"Erin."

"Okay, yes. I would not take Julian if I was planning my ride to the afterlife."

"Exactly. You don't believe it, either. The afterlife."

"I'm more open minded than I was," Erin said. "That's because of you. I want it to be true."

"The next time Father Mark comes in for a Guinness, tell him that. He'll put in a good word for me."

"Like you need it. Save them for the rest of us."

Leigh reached across the table and took Erin's hand. "You do know that Julian flirts with you, right? That he's just not very good at it."

Erin flushed with red. "I never... I didn't... really." she stammered to a halt.

Leigh leaned toward Erin and whispered, "It's okay to like Julian." She leaned back and resumed in her normal tone. "I'm prejudiced, but I think you'd be crazy if you weren't at least a little in love with him."

"How can you say that about me?"

Leigh smiled. "That comment was about him. More, the way I see him, I guess. No night vision goggles needed." She took a breath, having said what she needed to say. "I didn't mean to offend you or accuse you of anything."

Her skin returning to normal, Erin said, "You didn't. I think he's great. I love you both, so much. Can I leave it at that?"

"Of course. I just wanted you to know I how I feel about it. This may be my last chance."

From her eyes, Leigh knew Erin understood. Before Erin's eyes brimmed over, Leigh said, "I need one more favor.

"Okay?"

"You see the angel head?" Leigh gestured to the irritated angel affixed to the porch's brick wall, a plant on its Halo.

"It looks kind of mad."

"Thanks. I made it myself. About four years ago, right after..."

"Okay."

"It was therapeutic. I dumped every bad feeling I had into it. Julian wanted me to get rid of it after the operations, and the chemo seemed to work," Leigh went on. "But I knew it would come back. And I only had one in me. Too bad it was that vengeful one." She did not breathe for a moment and then forced a deep breath. "That hurt, believe it or not."

"I'm so sorry."

"That's the least of my worries," Leigh said. "Anyway, when we decided to hide a spare key, that cranky angel seemed likely to spook any would-be thieves. Would you check it for me, please?"

Erin rose and went toward the angel halfway and stopped. "She looks so mad."

"She has a fake plant on her halo all day. Every day. Better to think of it that way than to remember I had all that... what? Rage? Resentment? Inside me?" She laughed lightly. "And that was before chemo."

Erin approached the angel head and lifted the plant. She found nothing. "Your key is missing."

"That would be too easy," Leigh said. "It's behind the head. Tilt it. There is a recess. You'll feel it."

"I'm not sure I want to dig around in her."

"That's the point. Go one. She won't mind."

Erin followed directions and felt for the key. "Got it." She showed it to Leigh.

"Good. I want you to know where it is..."

"But Julian knows where it is. He won't get locked out."

Leigh laughed slightly. "He probably could, but that's not the point." She waited.

"I don't understand the point."

"I want you to know because I'm afraid Julian will lock himself in."

"Why would he do that?"

"I expect him to. It is his inclination – our inclination – and I know he'll withdraw further," Leigh said. "It is okay for a little while. He's on notice, though. One year of it is okay. But he can be stubborn. A year is enough."

Erin nodded, half of Leigh's meaning taking hold. "Oh. A year of mourning."

"He's in mourning now and doesn't realize it. He will probably deny it later, too, Leigh said. "Of course, Frank and Polly know about the key," Leigh added. "But you need to, too. I want you to know."

Erin waved the key in mock menace. "If he violates your rule, I'll come out here and get him, myself."

Leigh smiled. "That is the plan."

Erin stared at the key and began to grasp what it meant.

"You can put it back," Leigh said, rising from her chair. "But promise me you'll use it."

Erin slowly returned to the angry angel, took a breath, and put the key in place. When she turned, Leigh was looking at her with a satisfied expression. By the time Erin hugged Leigh as if it was the last hug of all time, she was sobbing.

"Don't cry, Erin. Go on, home," Leigh said, pushing Erin back enough to break the embrace. "It will be there when it's time."

Erin dried her eyes and kissed Leigh good-bye. Halfway to the car, she looked back, but Leigh was not visible. Erin did not look back again because she had to watch her unsteady feet.

Leigh had sat down as soon as Erin left the porch. She looked at the fierce angel.

It's my idea, and I'm jealous.

Not envy, jealousy.

Oh, God. What if I can see.

Having held together for hours, she gave way to shaking and tears. It took a while, but they did the trick.

The priorities of the day were complete.

Chapter Ten

August 2012

Leaning against the vanity, Leigh examined the Kleenex before she threw it away. The master bathroom wastebasket contained an empty tissue box and dozens of red and white sheets It was one-third. Her bedside basket accumulated more over the course of a day.

She had gone into the bathroom for a new tissue box for her bedside. She took one from the linen closet and counted the remainder. She still had plenty.

"Half a pallet worth," Julian had said upon returning from Costco.

"I plan to use them all," she had lied.

She took another tissue and wiped her pale lips. The color of her lips surprised her. The mirror reflected how she felt: Her eyes were slightly bloodshot, and her pallor was a light gray.

We need cheerier light bulbs.

She took a gulp of the appropriately-named vodka.

Spelling be damned.

"I admit it," she called to Julian, who sat on the bed. "It is darker."

"Should we call Dr. Morgan?"

Leigh opens the top vanity drawer. She knew the contents by heart, but the sight of half a dozen pill bottles reassured her. She had a larger cache under the kitchen sink. Over time, she had stockpiled. Vicodin and Valium were her personal favorites because of the alteration. She had Oxycontin, Percocet, Xanax. Paxil, Zoloft, and miscellaneous medications, too, to treat pain, anxiety, depression and insomnia. She was still a chemical experiment, despite dropping out of her personal chemotherapy trials.

She had filled every prescription, but, thus far, had used about half. Generally, she found she could get by, but all the conditions were getting worse, pain the clear leader. Vicodin still worked best for her, alteration or not.

"It's like I'm rusting on the inside," she said, forcing a laugh and shaking a couple Vicodins loose. "No, that's not the color. I'll have to consult my PPG Paint swatches."

"You are such a *homer*. Why not Sherwin-Williams?" He had asked the same question when Leigh picked PPG paints for repainting both times. Sears was closer to them than any PPG Paint outlet.

"I admire your persistence. Or is it repetition?"

Leigh moved onto the Valium. She put a second dose of each on the vanity top. She returned the bottles to the drawer. She swallowed the two pills with the rest of the vodka and closed the vanity drawer. Her staple combination tasted terrible together. "Thank you for your support," she said to the combination.

"Leigh, we discussed this," Julian chided her. "No talking to the V's without a doctor present."

"I'm closer to talking to Deacon Ryan." As she spoke, she watched her face in the mirror for any giveaway. Leigh had never been an effective liar, but she was getting better, especially when she wasn't flat-out lying.

"That sounds like fun. Picking out a crack in a wall."

There was a break, a wince. She turned it into a put-upon smile. "Only you would put it that way."

"I think is romantic: We are destined to be hole-mates."

She rolled her eyes., but laughed. It hurt, but the line deserved the response. "You are *so* haunted, Julian Cochran. Better buckle up."

Leigh took a last look at her face. She pinched and patted her cheeks. Some color rose. She scooped the pills with her left hand, pinched her empty glass between its thumb and index finger. She put the tissue box under that arm and hit the light switch with her right elbow.

Eat your heart out, wholesome-sexy waitresses everywhere!

The new tissue box was the Scott brand, instead of Kleenex or Kirkland. Most people did not pay attention to the brand of tissue they purchased – everyone called facial tissue *Kleenex*, anyway – once it went into a shopping cart. Leigh and Julian did. Their professions centered on promoting and distributing branded products.

In Leigh's case, advertising had slowly become a former profession. Not that she should have been in, to begin with. She had gone to CMU for graphic design and with hopes of becoming a set designer for the theater or movies. Gibbons Marketing, a regional ad agency that sponsored the Public Theater had hired her on the spot after seeing her last set.

"Commercials have sets, too," her new boss at Gibbons had said. "Ads need layout. You've got the *eye*."

While her career was moot, Leigh worried about Julian and his job. She did not express her concern, worried it worry him which would worry her all the more. She did not have enough Zoloft or Xanax to handle that.

Leigh returned to the bedroom and put down her glass and pills. With a perfect free-throw motion, she shot her latest balled-up tissue onto her three-foot-tall wastebasket. It bounced off the middle of the heap and onto the bed. It rolled up against her laptop, which sat between Julian's and her mattress sites.

"That's sad."

Sitting, she said, "I just need a bigger basket."

"I can have a brand new thirty-gallon drum in here in twenty... No, figure forty-one hours." Julian counted on his fingers. "I'll do the routing as soon as I finish this Mulching Channel show."

"I am still a better shot than you ever were." She swung her legs onto the bed.

"That is sadder. It's like..." He looked at the TV. "It's like saying you can hoe better than I can."

"No, it's not. You once played basketball."

Julian looked at her with simulated sadness. "Are you saying we are not hoe-mates?"

"Please stop that. You know we are."

"I know that half of us are," he said. He pointed to the laptop screen. A large graphic window abutted a document window. The graphic was a long-legged egg, that had once been a Mrs. Potato Head. "Kudos on the gams. A major improvement. "

Leigh snapped up the balled tissue and sat it on the full wastebasket. She gave the pile a push. The pile barely compressed. "Hm." She put her laptop where it belonged. She showed Julian her pills and pointed to her empty glass.

"Okay," he said, getting up. "I will bring a *Glad* bag for your *set* shots." He kissed her as he went by.

"Thank you."

"The *Glad* bag or the kiss."

"Oh. Sorry. I was thinking of the vodka," she said. "The other two, too."

"In what order?"

She patted his arm. "Don't embarrass yourself."

Julian guffawed and disappeared.

Leigh turned her attention to the graphics program from Erin. It had, indeed, been a Godsend. It helped her with her basic drawings – art, itself, was not a forte – and laid out suggested 3D wire-line cages for each item in the animation. The program had hundreds of suggested bodies, faces, appendages and other objects to choose from. Once a *cage* was selected, the program would do the animation in a million ways, coordinating the times in the layout. Her timer program involved several objects. It would sync to standard music beats, too.

She was using *Teardrops on My Guitar* by Taylor Swift for the music sample. She owned the song, but it failed to make her playlist cut, being a second short. No Taylor Swift song had made the list, yet, so being the test song was Taylor's consolation prize. She hit the *play* button in the timer window and watched the egg dance, rather badly to the muted song.

It's for Julian, after all.

No way. That doesn't look *remotely right.*

She selected *to the beat* instead of *off-beat* and hit play. Egg swayed to the song Leigh sang in her head.

Julian returned with a frosty glass and handed it to her. She threw the pills into her mouth and gagged them down. "Yuk."

"Only a double Triple-V? Your stash can't be getting low."

"I'm still in good shape," she replied. Realizing how stupid that sounded, she added, "I mean I have plenty of pills. That's not what worries me."

"I'm sure you don't worry about what Dr. Morgan would say to your treatment regimen."

"I know what he said at first."

"And you told him you didn't want another doctor."

"The last thing he said anything about it was what worries me. I am building up too much tolerance to them."

"You did go through a lot of doctors."

"You know what I mean."

"I do."

She nodded toward her document window and the spreadsheet it contained. "This *recipe* is outdated already. It's going to take more pills. A lot more, at my current tolerance. And that means my stomach may not be able to handle everything."

"In a perfect world, your stomach would not have to worry about that."

"In a perfect world, my stomach would be worrying about acid reflux."

Leigh tipped the glass to drain the contents and puts it next to the lamp on her bedside table. She focused on her laptop, studying the various parts of the timer display: The movement of the main graphic of the egg and the ticking of countdown clock as it approached zero. She hit the *unmute* icon. *Teardrops* played for its last few seconds.

"Ta da!"

The timer app said, in Leigh's voice, "Ding! It's time, Julian." After a beat, it added, "Oh, Julian."

"What do you think, oh, Julian?"

"I think you stole Mrs. Potato Head, fleshed out her stick legs and hid her under a fake chicken shell," he said. "It's an outrage. Except for the legs."

"I call her Ms. Egg Head, now. That avoids all that trouble with trademarks, not to mention with feminists."

Leigh right-clicked on the timer program and opened a code window. She made two quick changes. "One thing, the legs were not long enough to be..." She smiled. "Realistic."

"I don't know how I missed that," Julian said. "Maybe, by refusing to think Mrs. Potato Head was real?"

Leigh hit the play button, and *Nothin' Bout Love Makes Sense,* by LeAn Rimes played quietly.

"You said that song was too short. Taylor's, too."

"It is. I'm in developer mode."

"Disappointing."

"I agree, but rules are rules."

Leigh fast-forwarded. "FF is for the developer only."

"Not me?"

"Uh. No."

The song ended, and the Timer's Leigh-voice exclaimed, "Ding! It's time Julian."

"Better?"

Julian nodded. "It's only half as humiliating. Can we just sit back and watch the Crack Hoe channel?"

"That sounds too urban." She switched to the document window. "Besides, I have to update my instructions."

"Oh, for me?"

"No," she said. "Yes. Maybe."

Leigh had composed detailed, step-by-step directions for her to follow in committing suicide. *Cheaper, quicker and more certain than the other chemo,* had been her rationale. It remained so. Her new problem was her fast-increasing tolerance to the medications and the alcohol. "I have to include variables for tolerance and weight to figure dosages."

"All bases covered," Julian said.

"That's only three."

"That's how many bases there are. In baseball, no one says Home Base?"

"Sorry. I wasn't thinking *baseball.*" She tapped the spreadsheet. "Ultimately, *fourth base* is the one that counts."

"Metaphorically true."

They lapsed into silence and looked at the spreadsheet. Leigh had titled it *Lily's List*. It had six different medications listed – seven since Grey Goose counted as a medicinal in Leigh's case – taken in multiple dosages in a number of different steps.

"I call this a recipe not a metaphor," she said.

"It's more whimsy, calling it Lily's List."

"Do you *not* understand the meaning of whim?"

"Isn't it lighthearted use of cats' names and their videos on the internet?"

"Hence, the *not.*" When he did not respond, she repeated the point. "For Lily, there were defined steps. For me, it's the same thing."

"I know," Julian said. "But you keep making it more complicated. You used to have nine steps. What is it now? You have fifteen now."

"I have to be careful." She paused. "It was when I could get by with lower dosages. I need higher doses of them, so I have to space them out. I have to stay alert and keep the pills down, or I'm..." "She searched for better phrasing but only added a word. "I'm not dead."

"I do prefer you that way."

"For now. That will... alter."

"These dosages will seriously alter your state."

"Permanent alteration is the goal."

"I'll need to be altered, too, if not as much."

"I know, but only a little, Julian," she said, her hand running through his hair. "I need you to be with me – I need that anyway – in case I can't make it through all the steps. I may not be able to make any of them if it gets bad."

"I'll be there."

"Because of nausea, I won't be able to try this twice, Julian," she explained. "There's no way, now that the dosages are so high. It will be a *one-time only* deal."

"I'll be there," he said again. Then he looked at Lily's list. "I'll need a copy. No way I can memorize all that."

"It will be on my laptop. I don't want it on your computer or the tablet. Or anything else," she added, very serious. "You could get in real trouble. You don't know about this. Remember that."

"That I can remember. You can't visit me in jail," he said, with a gentle smile.

"Oh, I would," she reassured him. "But I'll throw such a fit - and other things - it will be cheaper to let you go than exorcise your cell." She kissed him on the cheek.

"I almost believe you," he said, kissing her back.

~ ~ ~

Leigh knew her stomach was barely holding up its end and could not do so forever. Her need for medication, in pill and liquid form, had overtaxed it. She had tried to keep her usage minimal, but the pain kept getting worse. As resigned to her fate as she told herself she was, anxiety belied her bravery.

The medications worked faster and better with vodka.

Or am I just telling myself that?

As Julian had put it, "Forget it. It doesn't fucking matter. Do what you have to. It's not like you're a Presbyterian."

In the spring, they had purchased new lounge chairs for the porch. Leigh had trouble sitting on the bistro chairs, and their previous chairs had never been comfortable for long periods of sitting. Originally, they had a table between them, but Julian bought a second so that her laptop could have its own.

Leigh's side of the middle table held some pills and two glasses. One glass contained Iceberg Vodka - Leigh had decided that Grey Goose was too expensive, and that Iceberg went down as smoothly - the other an especially light Pinot Grigio. The wine remained untouched.

How decadent have I become?

"God, that burns all the way down" She had difficulty getting the words out. "And not in a good way."

"How about some water?"

"That's what I just drank, except in Russian," she said. "I can't waste a swallow on water. Not anymore. It burns, too. You can have my wine."

Julian moved it over to his side of the table. "Wouldn't want you to renege on me."

"I don't have time to do that." She croaked it as lightly as her throat allowed. Since it was loosening up, she had to move to a topic she had been putting off. "Julian, I think you should date Erin."

He did not respond at all at first. Then he turned in his chair and locked onto her eyes. "I beg your pardon."

"You like her. I know you do."

"What happens if I say... something like, *who doesn't*?"

"It's not a test."

"That means it *is* a test if you say it is *not* a test."

Leigh had rehearsed what she would say, and she pressed on. "I worry about you. I think you need a smart woman to be happy. And Erin is pretty, too."

"You need a job."

"I have one," she said. "Well, I guess I have two. The second is to make sure you will be all right after the first one."

"Two years. I'll be peachy. Not a second longer or fruitier."

"One year," she insisted. "And not peachy. Happy. Again."

"Is there a clause where I can say, *I don't want to be happy, again?*" His smile was unconvincing. He was irritated at her. "Hogging the pathos is unbecoming."

"Thank you for reminding me. I'd love to stop."

"I don't think you can enforce an agreement like this. It is unconscionable."

"It's not a contract. Think of it as a dying request."

"It's not in your will," he said. "I have that. I get everything – and thank you, by the way – and Erin is *not* mentioned."

"She is now."

"You can't make me be happy."

"Don't bet I can't."

"I've seen *that* in movies. It never ends well."

"True," Leigh agreed. "But this is real life. Things are much stranger in real life."

For a minute, they stared at each other. Julian's anger had dissipated, as Leigh knew it would. No matter what, he had never been able to stay angry with her, on the rare occasions she had given him a reason.

She laughed.

"You know," he said, smiling, "Dr. Morgan didn't say anything about your brain going. Everything else, maybe, but not that."

"Have you seen what I just... consumed?" she asked. "The whole point is my brain. Well, half of it."

"Right or left?"

"You know what I mean."

"Can you *consume* something?" Julian rarely mentioned words like food anymore. He talked around words that might trigger nausea or coughing.

"The *can?* Maybe. But what did you have in mind?"

"Two eggs, soft-boiled to perfection."

Leigh pointed to her laptop and its egg timer program. "Until this works, *perfection* is off the table."

Julian held up his left wrist. "I have a watch."

"You have many watches, Julian. A drawer full," she reminded him. "You forget to look at them."

"All right, then," Julian said. "Let's give it a run. The egg thing."

Leigh looked at him. The program was not finished. She had some fine-tuning and hosting issues, but it did work. "Tell me when the water is boiling. If it doesn't work, you'll never hear about it again."

"Deal."

With that, Julian hurried off the porch and into the kitchen.

Sure, he was out of sight, Leigh allowed herself a couple quick sobs. After that, she used a few tissues to dry her eyes. Then, she set the laptop on her lap. She lowered the volume and ran just the finale of the timer program.

"It's time, Julian," her voice said.

The thought hit her, harder than she would ever have expected.

It's been too late to deliver Julian's baby for a while.

That is the thought her voiced words conjured. She had put off the thought of children until it was too late. Julian had never cared, but, in the future, he might.

Cue Erin.

That gave her yet another idea: Use a version of Erin's voice for the timer.

As a test of the concept, she tweaked her own computer voice to sound quite different but retain a subliminal *Leigh* quality to it. She played the voice, and it sounded pretty bad, but less *boy or girl, pink or blue.* She could live with it for the trial run.

She reset the timer program and waited.

Finally, Julian called, "It's boiling."

She hit the app's play icon. Ms. Egg Head began to dance away the next three minutes.

Leigh turned her attention to her short playlist in a spreadsheet window. She had a separate tab for songs that were a second or two off of three minutes. She studied her woefully short list. Into her music editor, she loaded two discarded songs: *Tears on my Guitar* and *Don't Think About It,* by Darius Rucker, each only off by a second.

That's cheating.

She closed the program. It defeated the purpose of the playlist to tweak songs that were not the perfect length, so Taylor and Darius were out.

What is the purpose? Only to torment Julian? Or to help him cook?

Is there any purpose?

Leigh refused to let herself consider the philosophical. Cooking was the purpose, though tormenting Julian was always fun. He was so good-natured about torture.

Besides, it was for his own good.

His good is paramount, his happiness.

An awful idea popped into her head.

Do I really want Julian to be happy with Erin? With anyone?

Be happy without me?

Dazed by that thought, Leigh was jarred by her modified voice.

"Ding! It's time Julian."

She called as loudly as her limited lungs would allow. "Take her out, Julian."

Seconds later, he appeared at the door. "I did. I have to fix 'em up."

It worked.

The egg was frozen in a very unflattering dance pose.

I have to fix that look.

"I'll time you," she called.

"Oh, come on."

She started the egg timer again. It played *Let Me Take You in My Arms Again* by Neil Diamond, another one-second too-short song. It would be the last time it would play in the app. Leigh decided to lock in the playlist with three-minute songs.

It had been a lot of work to prepare the Egg time app. Leigh recognized it was only going to help Julian for the shortest of times. He did not eat eggs.

I was wrong.

The app is only for him because it is for me.

She thought of Erin again, in more ways that one. Her own time was limited. Erin was the perfect successor. Julian knew her and liked her. Erin was already in love with Julian. It was perfect.

She startled herself for the next two thoughts.

Will he love Erin only because he loves me?

Is that fair?

Is it what I want?

Chapter Eleven

August 2013

Julian used the tablet to pushed aside the riot of printouts on the porch's bistro table. He needed to clear space for the seventy-third through seventy-eighth ounces of coffee propping open his eyes. He realized that printouts would have as much value to him with coffee stains as without.

He rocked, holding the chair's back, and waited. The USB drives jutted out on either side like stubby wings. As he glanced between its screen and the tablet, he thought that if the USB wings worked, he would sail the laptop into the stratosphere.

To be closer to its owner.

The tablet, as always, displayed the correct time, the laptop its three-minute deficiency version. Both devices ran the time program running on auto-restart and on mute, seemingly unaware their times differed...

Artificial Intelligence being a long way off.

Julian sat down. He leaned the tablet against the table's edge and called up his list of time-corrective possibilities. He tapped and highlighted each line, his touch becoming a jab. He had used almost all the listed measures, some two or three times and almost all of his patience.

He seized the piece of paper on the top of the printout mess and skimmed it. The log of routines stared back at him, as the abyss might if printed out. He crushed the paper into a ball and launched it over the front half-wall and well short of the stratosphere. It clunked when it hit his car.

"Next time..." he threatened the laptop. "In the meantime,..." He put the laptop and the tablet to sleep. He could not bear soft-shoeing eggs for the moment.

Without thinking, Julian entered the same mode.

It took a monstrous clap of thunder to jerk him awake. As abrupt as his reaction was, it took a minute for his vision to clear. The laptop and tablet slept on.

"How many of your three-minute performances did I miss, Leigh?" he asked. "Patsy Cline. Maybe a *Bad, Bad Leroy Brown*?"

By reflex, Julian checked his watch. It was his silver-toned Wittnauer, his fourth watch in four days. He literally had a drawer full of watches, accumulated in a quest for the perfect timepiece.

"Does *perfect* mean one you would actually pay attention to," Leigh had said. Futile as it may have been, she purchased most of them as gifts. "You are like the emperor who keeps buying clothes he forgets to wear."

"I have a perfect grasp of the time it takes a container ship to reach Long Beach from Taichung."

"I don't know where that is, but I'll bet it takes a calendar, not a watch."

Julian checked the watch again. He and the devices before him had been asleep for hours.

With right and left index fingers, he touched the laptop's touchpad and the tablet's power button. After waking, each displayed the time, as their opinions dictated. The tablet agreed with his Wittnauer. The app windows...

On the laptop, the app did not reopen.

The tablet's app played merrily into the second half of ABBA's *When I Kissed the Teacher*.

"So, Leigh, your Limbo can't let go of ABBA any more than you could," he said, as he called up the laptop's background screen, its desktop. Julian started to say something, but it ended up being "what the fuck?" instead.

The app' Father Time icon was no longer on the laptop's desktop screen, either.

He felt a wave of relief. "Bye, bye, Pops."

A tsunami followed, and he sagged.

Have I lost you, too?

The tablet's egg danced on. He turned up the reassuring end of ABBA. Her program was alive and well, just not on the laptop.

Her laptop. Her program.

Their connection.

He had come to think of the laptop as it always had been: Leigh's. The timer app was the last thing she had done, and she had done it for him, for good or torture.

Without it, are you gone?

The song ended. On the tablet, the Egg jumped onto its shooter. When it jumped off, the laptop app opened and matched the tablet, but–

He could have sworn he had seen the phrase *Miss Me?* flash below the laptop's dancing Egg.

He blinked, long after the words had disappeared from the space that showed *Oh, Julian* when the app was muted.

Assuming they were there, to begin with.

Julian closed the laptop's lid and flipped it over.

This is fuck you *territory.*

His fingers fumbled while removing its battery. He waited through a chorus or two before he flipped it back and opened the lid. He fixed on the power button.

Ghosts don't need no stinkin' battery!

Julian pushed the power button. Nothing happened. He pushed it again. Nothing happened. He tapped it repeatedly. The screen remained black.

"Ding! Oh, Julian," said the tablet, in that unfamiliar familiar voice. If it had been Leigh's, however, modified, he would have known. It was not.

Why not? Why not give me that much?

The next song started, *Daydream Believer,* by Neil Diamond via the Monkees. Julian stared at the laptop as if had chosen the song intentionally.

He knew better It was not the laptop.

Chapter Twelve

August 2012

The 13-inch LCD TV from the kitchen was small enough to move to the porch whenever Leigh and Julian were desperate for, at that moment, something like the Travel Channel. It sat to the left of the angry angel head, on a sturdy tray table. The two of them sat at the bistro table, instead of their lounge chairs. The hard bistro chairs were more practical if not more comfortable. Leigh was working to finalize her *twisted magic* – her words, not Julian's, not that he disagreed – with the egg timer app.

She had just chosen its icon. An elderly Father Time, shouldering a scythe. He looked slower than Julian, explaining his win over a shapely hourglass with eye-blue sand. The shapely part was *so* not her. In third place, as too dull, was an egg in an egg cup backed by a small analog clock face.

She felt a flush of delight at finalizing the icon selection.

Good God, my bar is low.

Completing the project had become more important that the program itself or decent soft-boiled eggs.

Her drawn appearance, short breathing, a speckled pile of used tissues and obvious weakness spoke for her.

Though he could see the filing wastebasket and her decline, Leigh felt Julian was not ready to hear how she felt.

That was about the scythe of it.

Damn. I sound like Julian.

The laptop's two document windows showed her *cheat sheet* of songs with lengths from 2:58 to 3:02 minutes. The sheet had a separate section for the official playlist already programmed in to accompany, randomly, the dancing egg. She liked playing the off-list songs outside of the app. It had taken a lot of effort to find and download them, too.

Leigh had set up one of the 2:59-minute songs to play, the Go-Go's *Vacation*. She thought it would be funny while watching a Travel Channel centered on the elaborate private homes around Cannes, France.

"Those damned French know how *vacation hideaways*," Julian said. Sex on a private Mediterranean beach."

"Sex on any beach," Leigh countered, with a shadow of a laugh.

"Sex anywhere."

"My romantic husband."

"Directly quoting his romantic wife."

She sighed. "It isn't you. Or me. It's this damned body. Everything feels wrong."

"The Travel Channel with you is all I need."

Vacation stopped playing without a *Ding*!

"I like that song," she said.

"Is it in the app?"

"It's a second too short."

"One lousy second. It's the Go-Gos, for God's sake." Julian glanced the unapproved list. "Balance it out with that Green Day at three minutes plus."

"Sorry. Present company excepted, I resolved to stick to my standards."

"Thanks. Wait."

She waited.

"Have you looked?" he asked. "A different version may be longer."

Leigh closed her eyes and put her head back. "Oh, wow. How could I be so dumb?" She looked at him, with a smile. "Do you want to answer that?"

"I doubt it."

She looked back at her outlier list. "I did find a Karaoke version."

"That would be wrong."

"That's what I decided." She laughed and coughed. "I looked. Amazon, Google, iTunes. That song is always 2:59. *Basket Case* is always 3:01."

She hit the play key for the next song on the *excluded* list, bringing up *Shilo* by Neil Diamond.

"To give you an idea of what I've gone through," she said. "*Shilo* is 3:01 on one album and 2:59 on another. I mean, help me out, Neil!"

"He always seemed so empathetic, too."

Leigh closed the playlist text file. The icon representing it appeared: An angel face, with an *O* for a mouth, framed by wings and a halo.

"Don't look now, Leigh, but something just flew out from the living room."

"I'm covering all my bets."

"I never saw you as superstitious –"

"How dare you!" she cried, feigning outrage. "I'm a good Irish Catholic girl."

"Okay. That explains Mrs. Potato head, but you don't even knock wood. Even I do that."

"You're a pagan atheist," she said. "Did I try to change you?"

Julian knocked on the steel table, three times.

"Pagan atheists have *no* standards."

"So, wait. Do you exclude me from your nightly prayers?"

"Uh..."

"Oh, my God. You do."

Leigh fought off a giggle with painful effort, which still stole some breath. "I pray for you and me. For more time together. Quality time, like this... with fewer dumb questions."

"Just one more," he said. "You never pray for just me? My soul?"

"Indirectly, yes, I do. I pray that I will not have to suffer watching you live alone... Without repartee. Not for very long."

"So being about *me* is really about *you*. Hmm."

She looked away, hiding the reinforcing impact of his words. She kept her sigh shallow, nonetheless. "I'm sorry. I can't separate us very well." To shift the topic to safer ground, she said, "The problem with praying? It's called *asking for too much*."

"Where does Erin fit in?"

Between us, temporarily.

Leigh almost choked on the thought.

Get a hold of yourself.

"I mean prayer-wise."

"Oh. I tried praying that you would marry her and live *happily* ever after. I mean after... You know." She shrugged. "For a few years, after."

"That's some prayer, you've got there."

"I tried, but it's not a good idea to display jealousy when praying. It makes the process longer."

"You are the least jealous person I've ever met."

"Julian," she said, earnestly. "I'm not the person I was. Not half. Not a third. My only confidence is that I will die. I'm jealous of about six billion people."

"It's nice you can fit Erin in."

"I real terms, I can't think beyond a few months," she said. "That can be why I talk about her… a year out. As of now, I can live with that." She laughed.

"Not to muck up a nice plan," Julian said, locking her eyes, "but, assuming I can be happy with Erin, I won't love her. I can't even try."

Leigh wanted to throw her arms around him, but she did not want to screw up the nice plan. "That is an acceptable compromise," she said, matching her conflicting feelings. She barely restrained letting it out what she felt.

He is too wonderful!

Chapter Thirteen

August 2013

In the nearly a year since Leigh died, Frank and Julian had *done* lunch at Renegades. Julian had not been on the same street. It was, to him, Leigh's street.

Frank blackmailed Julian into meeting him at Renegade's. Frank promised to help Julian with his laptop problem on the condition they revisit their usual place. Unable to justify his avoidance, Julian agreed, but not for lunch, on the grounds that he did not eat lunch any longer.

Julian picked a time well after Erin's lunch shift would end, *for many drinks* and technical advice.

Things went south the moment they walked past the restaurant's window. Erin stood at a window-side table taking an order. She looked, it seemed, unusually attractive.

Julian stopped dead in his tracks.

A perfectly good plan shot to hell.

Frank stopped, too, but he waved to catch Erin's attention.

Erin looked out, and her eyes snapped open wide. She managed a brave smile that remained though her eyes grew closer to tears. She turned abruptly and left the table.

This is already going so *well.*

Frank and Julian had their choice of booths, only the last two being occupied. They chose a middle booth. Julian sat first, facing the window. He swung the laptop onto the table as soon as he was seated.

A short, thin waitress Julian recognized as Donna came over to the table. Like Erin, she wore the tight jeans and belted shirt uniform of Renegades, but unlike Erin, she did not do the outfit justice.

When he first saw the contrast, Julian felt relief. That feeling ran smack into disappointment, fracturing into other emotions. The truth was that finally close to contact, he was anxious to see Erin. The dread he had felt for almost a year also intensified. He did not want Leigh to be right, that he was, had been, attracted to Erin.

It did not help matters that she wore more make-up than he had ever seen, done perfectly. She also had two-inch heels instead of flats or sneakers.

The jumble of feelings added up to a conflicted *glum*.

Leigh's plan for Julian and her insistence on it had bothered him from the start.

Now, this.

Julian's Grey Goose and Frank's Jack Daniels, each on three rocks, came quickly. The waitress had just asked if they wanted a menu when Julian ordered a second vodka. He handed over his empty glass.

"If that is how it is to be," Frank said, tossing his Jack back, "I accept the challenge."

Julian booted up the laptop. He took out his phone. "Take out your phone, Frank."

"Oh. Yeah, okay."

Julian had briefed Frank on his struggles with the laptop. Frank had sounded skeptical but, on that one condition of location, had volunteered to help.

"Hi." Erin sounded strained. She put down their drinks.

"Well," Frank said. He patted the seat next to him,

"Hi, Julian." She did not wait for a reply before she slid beside Frank.

"Now, that's the service I expected." Frank's eyes glinted with the success of his conspiracy.

Julian forced himself to meet her eyes. He saw them mirrors of his own, full of fear, elation, trepidation, guilt. He looked at his glass, lifted it and took a slug. His throat was not ready, and he coughed out, "Hi, Erin."

Erin looked as decimated as she felt.

Frank jumped in to ease the tension. He put his hand over Julian's glass. "Now. Try that again."

The ploy had the desired – and a visual – effect. "I'm sorry." Julian smiled. "Hi, Erin."

"Hi." She beamed back, realized it and backed off to a smile. "You've been missed. Or is it missing?"

"Thanks."

"And yes," Frank said. "I've had him on milk cartons for months. There have been occasional sightings. Though, that may have been Big Foot."

"He's taller, and I've been at your house three times."

"Oh. I thought you had sent a clone. Set on mute. Hm. So, that was you?"

"Sorry if I forgot to get drunk enough to get a word in."

"I'm glad to know it wasn't me." Relaxed by the banter, Erin had spoken without thinking.

A strained laugh escaped Julian's lips.

"I didn't mean that the way it sounded. I meant I was so used to you guys... Every week. You tipped so well –"

"I still do. Julian? We'll see. Today's his tab."

Julian was not up to a rejoinder. His emotional processor was busy.

"I was kidding. It's almost a year since..." Her eyes opened wide, closed and barely opened again. Her voice was soft. "I mean since... you've been here."

Frank said, "I'm working Julian back into society. This was the place to start. Mostly, you, of course."

"I feel better. Thanks, Frank." She kept her confused eyes on Julian. "I'm happy you're back."

"Happy to be here," Julian said, unconvincingly. He shrugged. "Things have been a little crazy lately, I needed Frank's help with something. He wanted to come here. I'm glad we did. It's good to see you."

"I'm glad. I have missed you. Both of you."

"It wasn't easy," Frank said. "I had to pry him off his porch with a laptop. That laptop."

She broke eye contact and glanced at the laptop.

Julian shuddered. He finished drink number two. "True."

"It's Leigh's." Erin looked at Frank. "Is there something wrong with it?" Her eyes returned to Julian's, her voice became wistful. "The last time I saw it, it was on that porch."

"You've been on our porch?" Julian let his surprise show. "When? How?"

"Only once," she said, suddenly annoyed.

"Oh."

"Yeah, oh." Erin outlined an eyebrow for a break. "Seriously. Do you think a girl like me needs to stalk some... retiring retiree?"

"Not hardly," Frank said.

"How about you, Julian. Is that what you think?"

"I would have invited you in," Julian said. "But the place is *already* chock full of angels."

Frank laughed. "Good recovery."

"I know it used to be," Erin said, a hash of emotions. "I can't imagine it still is. With just you." She slid out and picked up Julian's glass.

"Are you ready? For another?' she demanded. "Grey Goose, rocks."

"I don't know," Julian said, thrown by Erin's comment. "Frank?"

"I didn't ask him. Sorry, Frank. You, too?"

Frank looked at his full glass. "I'll be done when you get back."

"Me? *When*?" She glared at Julian, then at Frank. "I assumed you'd want Donna back."

Frank narrowed his eyes at her. "Sure. If that's easier for you."

She bristled. "You know, Frank. Nothing's been fucking easy for me. You, too," she snapped at Julian. "You... No." She turned to leave. Then she stopped and swung around. "I drove Leigh home last Summer if you must know. That's been it for me and your home. Your precious porch." She hesitated. "Lucky me. I'll be your waitress, today." She stomped away.

For the next full minute, Frank and Julian said nothing. It was the longest time in their very long friendship.

"My fault," Frank said. "Not hers."

The comment took Julian by surprise. "Fault? What fault?"

"I asked her to change shifts," Frank admitted. "But I didn't tell her why. I knew it was risky, but I thought it would help get you out of your... *place*. I didn't know about hers."

"Place? What place is that?"

"The place we call nutsville. Yeah, I'm the one who's been visiting you there." Frank closed the laptop. "You gotta get out more." His gesture included the whole of Renegade's. "Hence..."

"You're right."

"I remembered Erin as bright sunshine. You do need a tan."

"She *is*. It's my fault." Julian sighed. "Besides, the tan can wait." He tapped the laptop. "This other curse can't."

Frank wondered about the odd use of the word *other* but decided to ignore it in favor of Julian's pressing computer problem. "Okay. Open her... it up."

First, Julian woke up his phone and moved it next to the laptop. His hand quivered. "Your phone, too. I want you to really see... this thing."

"Okay. Okay. Calm down." He dug out his phone and laid it on the other side of the laptop.

Julian opened the laptop, and it came alive. "The time. See?"

Frank first looked for the time on the taskbar. "Where..." He saw the analog clock face and digital readout. "Oh."

"It's the operating system's time. I checked a dozen times."

"Still." Frank opened the time routine and checked the system time and reactivated the taskbar display." He glanced at each phone in turn and back to the laptop. He killed the taskbar display. "Okay. It's a laptop with a busted clock that looks like a clock only in aqua."

"If only."

"Come on, Julian. It's electrons and software."

"It's three fucking minutes. Why? Three minutes."

"That, I can't explain."

Julian leaned forward and whispered, almost hissed. "The Navy clock, you know the Navy clock site. I've done it twelve times. It worked, then it didn't." He leaned back and said, normally, "Twelve times."

"Thank God. Thirteen would mean obsession." He gave Julian a bit of a smile.

Julian smiled back. He opened his clenched hands. "Whew. Wouldn't want that."

"So, how does it work?" Frank asked. "You managed to change the time, sync it with just about any clock, manually or automatically. Right?"

"Repeatedly."

"It works in the time routine, any time-set routine. And then it reverts to the three minutes."

"Immediately."

"I see your point." Frank took out a blue envelope and a pen. He began to scribble notes.

Julian watched Frank's hand, saying nothing, but wondering if anyone could read Frank's handwriting. He did notice something and whispered, "Is that a Viagra envelope?"

"What if it is? It's not like I need a solicitation."

"It means something is going last longer than three..."

Erin's voice, more normal, finally, asked, "Did you *finally* miss me?"

"Erin–"

"I admit it," Frank said, his hand out as he focused on his notes.

"I can *so* tell." She put the glass in his hand, supporting it until she was sure he had it. When she faced Julian, her eyes and cheeks were pink. "I'm sorry," she said. "Really. I guess I thought you'd be happier to see me."

"I hide it well," Julian said. "This last year has been completely lost."

"Mine, too," she said. She put Julian's drink down, avoiding his phone. "But not as bad. I can't pretend–"

"Pity parties," Frank said, still jotting notes, "are distracting."

Erin and Julian glanced at Frank and then each other.

"He's right," Julian said. "Party's over.

"Okay, then. What is so much more important than me?"

Frank looked up from the paper at her. "We have no idea."

"Why thank you."

"And we have no idea."

She peered at his notes. "Is that Sanskrit... Uh oh. Is that a Viagra solicitation?"

"Don't be silly," Frank said.

"Don't be silly which?"

"You are very unlikely to find both Sanskrit and Viagra at Happy Hour."

"It's not Happy Hour."

"Aren't you happy?" Frank asked, discretely glancing from her eyes to Julian and back.

"I'm getting there," she said. She heard her name. She put her hand on Julian's shoulder and when he looked up at her, said, "Gotta go. I'm in demand."

Once she was gone, Frank said, "Be advised, Julian. She's in demand."

"She should be." He wiggled the laptop. "This thing, not so much. Why is it three minutes? Why not 2:59? Like the Go-Gos?"

"How did the Go-Gos get into a 2013 conversation?" he asked before he realized. "Oh, Leigh's playlist. They're on it."

"They missed by one fucking second."

"That's harsh. What song?"

"Frank. It doesn't matter," Julian snapped. He relented. "*Vacation*."

"One second and you miss out on a young Belinda Carlyle? No wonder you're such a mess."

Julian clutched Frank's arm and let it go immediately. "It makes no sense. Three minutes?"

"Coincidence."

"Or some kind of punishment."

"Computers do not punish people. Except in *2001*."

"See."

"No, Julian. It's not a punishment. For what?"

Julian said nothing. They both knew Julian had been too late.

"Okay. Maybe, it's a message," Julian said, feeling a burden lifting. Until that moment, he had been alone, with no one to bat his loony ideas back at him. "That makes more sense."

"Sense is being overused here, Julian. You do know that?"

"It's a message?"

"It's a glitch, Julian. For Christ's sake. They happen all the... a lot."

"Okay, then we have to fix it," Julian said. "But if we can fix it... I don't know what that means."

"Sure, you do."

"It means no message," Julian conceded. "Just a glitch."

"I think it is the CMOS battery going. Something temporal like that.'"

"CMOS would be gradual."

"Usually," Frank hemmed.

"Not usually. Time would go off gradually, a few second at a time," Julian said. This was three minutes. In an instant. A CMOS battery wouldn't do that. A complete CMOS failure, and I have no boot."

"All right. I agree." Frank rubbed the bridge of his nose and closed his eyes. "I got nothing off the top. But I will take it apart get to the motherboard and–"

Julian reached across and grabbed Frank's arm again. He did not let go. "No! You can't do that!"

"Sure, I can. I do it all–"

"No. I mean, you can't. As in I don't want you to."

Frank took Julian's hand off him. "I'm using that."

"Not very well."

"Look. I know what Leigh was to you. I do. But this is a notebook computer we are talking about. It's not her. Souls can't live on silicon alone. Look it up."

"Where?"

Frank laughed. "Google. That's all I've got."

"I think I've used that to my limit."

"Whatever it going on, it is not a message to you from her. I'm sorry."

"Then we can fix it."

Erin had been listening to the last part of the conversation, but neither man had noticed her. "Fix what? Can I help?"

"No, no. Erin, thanks," Julian blurted. "Thanks."

"It's computer stuff," Frank explained. "Down to the motherboard stuff."

"Not my forte." She fixed her eyes on Julian.

"Mine, either," Julian said. "As it turns out."

"When you're ready, Julian," she said softly. Then she stiffened, embarrassed at the sound of the words. "As in burgers, not drinks, I mean." She looked at their full glasses. "You need food before you have another drink."

"Bacon cheeseburger, fries," Frank said.

Julian was focused on the laptop.

"Julian?"

Julian did not respond.

After a couple beats, Franks said, "Try again. With emphasis."

"Oh, Julian?" Erin asked with a lilt.

He started. "Oh, shit," he whispered. It was the voice. It was not the voice, but it *was* the voice. "Oh, shit, Erin. I'm so sorry. It's this damned laptop. It's driving me nuts. I'll have what Frank's having. But I'll need another drink. Right now."

Leigh had used Erin's voice for the damned Egg app. That was, for sure, a message.

Chapter Fourteen

August 19, 2012

Julian may not have been proof of the *watched pot never boils* maxim, but he might have been Exhibit One supporting the theory that a *not watched pot will keep over-boiling if you don't watch the time.*

He sat against a bolster watching the three-minute countdown on the tablet. In the mattress valley to his left, Leigh tapped rapidly into a document. She kept the laptop skewed so that he could not read the text from his angle.

"Boy, you're busy."

"Details, Julian. Last minute, private details." Her voice did not invite a response.

"Can I help?" he asked anyway.

She shot him an annoyed look but immediately softened. "Sorry. No. It's not..." She sought the right words. "Just some notes I don't want to share. Not right now. Maybe, later."

"Hey. I'm just the husband and egg cooker."

"Much, much better at one than the other." She went back to typing.

As he listened to Maroon Five perform a low volume version of *Give a Little More,* perfectly synced, from the two devices' speakers, Julian admitted, internally, that he bore the blame for the egg dancing on the screens. Leigh may have created the annoying app, but he had created the need, given her the idea.

Almost all the songs, too, he acknowledged, were good to very good, some reaching classic status.

Neither of them looked as good as the music. Julian stubble had become post-stubble. His pallor was off, and his eyes rimmed in the same red as Leigh's. Her posture, alone, told her tale, but shallow, raspy breathing underscored it. The half-full wastebasket weighed in, as well.

Nonetheless, Leigh concentrated on the laptop. He understood that it helped her deal with her declining condition.

"Ms. Egg Head has good taste," Julian said. "If only in music."

Leigh shrunk the Excel window. She moved the laptop forward in her lap and shook her head. Then she slid the laptop down to her thin upper thighs. Then, she crushed a key and waved her arm in the air. "I was jealous of her, so... I put myself in the laptop, too." She angled the laptop slightly. "I'll be lost if I move it too much. Lean over."

Julian ran some reports through his head, using *lost*, and every single one dismayed him. He leaned a bit toward her, instead. At that angle, the LCD screen was washed out, but he could see Leigh's image in a large, left-hand window.

She waved, and the image waved. She pulled him closer and held him there for a few seconds, staring at the screen. "We look so... us... together," she said, mostly to herself. "Just like always."

"Except who's that scumbag with you?"

Leigh pushed him away, and his image slid from the screen.

It looks so wrong, me without Julian.

She hid her anxiety. "I have to admit, the picture could use *cleaner* details on the right, but I still found it beautiful."

"Leigh, you find properly arranged boxes beautiful."

"And people." She looked at herself on the screen again. "One, solo, does not look right, that's for sure."

"That one does," he said with a laugh. "But I liked the two better. I always have."

Leigh felt the unwelcome uncertainty spreading and changed the subject. "Why didn't I figure out this video thing sooner?"

"Because I didn't *egg* you on?"

With a sincere grimace, she said, "You *have* to get more sleep."

"True."

"Okay, watch this." She hit a stop icon at the bottom of the video window. With a couple keystrokes more, paused the egg timer program and ran the previous twenty seconds in video, complete with their voices and Maroon Five competing with itself a half a minute off, on the tablet. She paused it on their faces.

In her first glance at the image, her uncertainty surged.

What if I've been wrong?

Julian rubbed his chin. "I wonder how I would look on YouTube with a beard?"

She glanced at him and then the screen. "We don't have to wonder. You look pretty awful."

"And you look awfully pretty."

Leigh started to respond and did not. She knew how she looked, face drawn, eyes puffy, lips white.

Pretty, as in pretty bad.

She knew how she felt inside and it was not even that good. Fortunately, Julian had no idea. No one could. "You're wonderful. In so many respects, the truth not one of them. The beard look is another."

It's us. That is *wonderful.*

Stop thinking that!

"I'll shave when the eggs are done," he said. "Then you can seat us properly. We want to look our best for *YouTube."*

"This is not for *YouTube*, Julian," she said, kissing his cheek. "Just for you."

"Then, I don't have to shave?"

"You do, but you don't have time," she said, seriously. She pointed to the tablet. The countdown clock went under one minute. She ran the laptop version again, and it jumped to the same place in time and song.

"I'd rather be here with you."

Yes.

"And I'd rather try to eat one last time if that's okay." She winced at her phrasing.

I don't know. Not anything.

He got up, carrying the tablet, and walked around the bed. He tried to kiss her on the lips, settling for a cheek. "It's not."

"I didn't mean it. Not that way." She smiled as much as she could. "Please. Go. Take the eggs out when the app dings. It will reset, and you have a leisurely three minutes to de-shell them, butter them and get them up here. That is plenty of time for a normal human."

"Assuming I'm merely normal."

"Assuming you have the tablet with you," she said. "Forty-five seconds. Do not fiddle, Julian. I do want you back here with me, but mostly... I don't like cold soft-boiled eggs."

"Me, either."

"Go."

After jogging in place for two seconds, Julian finally left the room. She heard his feet take the stairs quickly. His departure depressed her.

She looked herself, alone, on the laptop screen.

Don't leave me alone, Julian.

She covered the pathetic face on the screen. She smiled in spite of how she felt. She tried to laugh the feelings off.

She grabbed a tissue, optimistic that she would catch the fluid that would result, in all its dark red glory.

Right on both counts.

She reopened the Excel window and hesitated. She had Horizontally merged cells above and below her table of meds, allowing full word-wrap, so that she could type in the text as if it were in Word. She had instructions at the bottom and a short note at the top. She looked at the note.

It isn't right.

She did not want to do it. It took all her strength not to call Julian to her side, right then. *That* is where he belonged.

Time for me to say so.

Leigh began talking as she typed. She opened her File Transfer Protocol program, giving access to her ftp site.

~~~

With the tablet softly singing him on, Julian made it fifty feet to the kitchen in record time. He congratulated himself only as long as it took to remember that returning would be much slower. After months of inactivity, his leg muscles had atrophied. He could not easily take the steps two at a time any longer.

He lay the tablet down beside a slotted spoon. An adjoining cereal bowl contained ice water. He had already positioned the requisite paper towels, butter, pepper and sea salt. The countdown timer was at fifteen seconds. He grabbed the slotted spoon, poised it above the boiling water to–"

"Ow! Fuck!" He traded the spoon to his left and put his right in the ice water. "She'll never know," he whispered to the dancing egg. "If you stick to singing or whatever."

The timer hit zero. "Ding! Oh, Julian." He could hear it from the bedroom as well as the tablet.
~~~

The time app reset and started again, this time with Elvis's *Can't Help Falling in Love*."

He took out one egg and then the other. "I've got 'em!" he called out, setting the second in the ice water. Cooling the eggs would take at least a third of his allotted time. From painful experience, he knew that hot eggs took much longer to handle. "Three minutes–" He glanced at the app. "Two forty-three, two. To go."

Leigh called something back. Her voice was weak and muffled. Still, Julian was fairly certain she had not said, "Take your time."

Thanks to the egg timer app, he knew exactly how much time he had been given.

Chapter Fifteen

August 2013

The indexing and searching programs sorted through thousands of files on both the laptop and the desktop, including hidden and system files. The desktop, though older, was much faster at processing than the laptop. On the other hand, it contained many, many more files. The first dozen times he had indexed the files, the two computers had would up in a dead heat.

Luckily, as the thirteenth ran at 2:15 AM, neither machine seemed any more ready for sleep than Julian.

Julian was running the searches to–

Cue the irony–

The laptop's egg timer app had vanished on the way back from Renegade's.

His initial applause had faded quickly.

Come back!

He knew irrational behavior when he observed it, but he had to find it. The laptop's onboard search routine was too basic. Julian bought more, five in all for both the laptop and the desktop. Leigh's app had to be somewhere.

Julian sat back and looked at the two screens. The desktop timer app ran as usual, with *Notion* by the Kings of Leon providing the desktop's egg-dancing music.

With a deep sigh, he ran his fingers through is hair. He looked at his palms for traces of grease. At least, none was visible. His hair reminded him. He rubbed his jawline.

He had really let himself go.

Come on! Let's pity party!

Fortunately for him, the search programs needed no intervention after he put in the keywords. Half aware, he watched the egg timer program run on the desktop. He pulled out his mobile phone and checked the app on it. He rarely looked at the phone. He made and took very, very few calls and Skype on his desktop sufficed for that purpose.

The time display matched the desktop, as usual.

Once the app was open on the phone, it also matched the desktop, in every respect, egg, dance, song and tick of the countdown. He put the phone back in his pocket. He checked his watch. He had set the Rado to match the internet time to the hundredth of a second, quite a feat even for an obsessive.

He undid the watch and walked into the near bedroom. The top left drawer of the short dresser contained his watch drawer, which, in turn, contained a dozen watches, all gifts from Leigh.

He took out a Seiko and checked its time against the Rado. They matched to the extent he could tell with the Seiko's hands. The Rado went in the drawer, the Seiko on his wrist.

By the time he returned to the office, the indexing segments of the utilities had concluded. He typed in *timer*; *playlist*; *egg; Ms. Fucking egg head.* He deleted the second, as he did not believe the term *playlist* would lead him to the app itself. He hit *search* on both computers.

He had searched *Lily* and came up with hundreds of files, most of them photos. Impossibly, no search had returned *Lily's List,* not even on the laptop. It seemed unlikely Leigh had bothered – or had time – to delete the *recipe* spreadsheet. He put that oddity aside, as immaterial.

"Come on, give me something," he begged the search programs. "I know it's in there."

The search windows, once again, showed absolutely nothing.

His glaring at the results had no effect on the results.

Can I waterboard a laptop?

The *IM* tone startled him. It was a video incoming from Jill on the laptop. Julian had deactivated video chats, for obvious reasons: He looked like hell, and Jill had harped mercilessly on his appearance.

JIL – *Good morning, Julian.*
JUL – *Not really, Cuz.*
JIL – *Was that intended to be surly?*
JUL – *Just exasperated. All-nighter.*
JIL – *Not to nag, but that's not good.*
JUL – *It also turned out to useless.*
JIL – *I just wanted to know what you wanted me to do.*
JUL – *Pet a cat and have a nice day?*
JIL – *I will and I will, but I mean about the file you sent me.*
JUL – *File?*
JIL – *Yeah. File.*
JUL – *What file?*
JIL – *Egg.Timer.ftp.doc*

Julian watched as his hands began to shake and waited for it to spread. It made it all the way to his head in record time.

JIL – *Julian?*
JUL – *When the fuck did you get it?*

JIL – *Whenever an asshole the fuck sent it?*
JUL – *Sorry. I am, but I didn't.*
JIL – *Didn't what?*
JUL – *I didn't send anything to anybody.*
JIL – *Yes you did.*
JUL – *All I do is search for answers these days.*

As he saw the line repeated in the *IM* window, he knew she would have a smart-ass comeback. She surprised him.

JIL – *I got it at 4:22 AM.*
JUL – *This AM?*
JIL – *Yes. That's why I'm here.*
JUL – *From me?*
JIL – *Yes, Julian. It was attached to an IM from the laptop.*
JUL – *From this laptop?*
JIL – *If it was George Clooney's, well, nice knowing you.*
JUL – *What did it say?*
JIL – *It said Attached. Just that.*
JUL – *That sounds like me, does it?*
JIL – *I was surprised. And you never used Leigh's laptop to IM me.*

Julian realized that he had stopped breathing, but it took a cough to remind him. He never used Leigh's laptop to do anything... except to play eggs and reset time.

JUL – *I didn't, Jill.*
JIL – *Didn't what?*
JUL – *Send it.*
JIL – *Yes, you did.*
JUL – *Right hand to God.*
JIL – *Try again. More realistic this time.*

JUL – *Okay. Honest. I didn't.*
JIL – *You didn't, like, lose the memory in that fog over there.*
JUL – *I was on it all night, running searches. Until just now.*
JIL – *Oh.*
JUL – *I didn't send shit.*
JIL – *No way.*
JUL – *Way.*
JIL – *No way.*
JUL – *In fact, way, way way.*

The pause between messages drew out. Jill was usually lightning quick.

JIL – *The ghost in the machine.*

Jill believed in *things*, but, like Leigh, rarely mentioned the things to others, except, occasionally, Julian or Leigh. She did coin *Pagan Atheists* for Julian and Frank, one of Leigh's favorite oxymorons.

JUL – *That's one theory. The leading one.*
JIL – *Coming from you, that's scary.*
JUL – *Did you open it?*
JIL – *I just got up.*
JUL – *Slacker!*
JIL – *I only IM'ed to razz you about another all-nighter.*
JIL – *And please stop those.*
JUL – *I will.*
JUL – *Please don't open that file.*

Julian sought the best approach to restrain Jill's supernatural curiosity.

JUL – *It must be a hoax.*

JUL – *Maybe malware. Opening it may fuck up your machine.*

JUL – *Send it to me. I'll deal with it.*

JIL – *Sold.*

JIL – *It's on its way.*

Julian stared at the screen, waiting, anticipating, wanting, perhaps, a message more than an answer. He opened his file manager window and navigated to the desktop's *Downloads.*

Sure enough, there it was: Egg.Timer.ftp.doc.

JUL – *Got it. Thank you. Bye.*

JIL – *Get some sleep, asshole. Bye.*

Julian closed the IM window and concentrated on the file manager. He had never seen that file name. Leigh had never mentioned it. He had never paid attention to the names of Leigh's files, except for Lily's List, for obvious reasons.

He typed *Egg.Timer.ftp.doc* into the laptop search program. He waited a full minute, knowing and getting the result of *not found*. He tried *ftp.doc* with the same outcome.

The downloads window and Egg.Timer.ftp.doc seized his full attention. Its doc extension distinguished it from a docx file, the current Microsoft Word version. A *doc* file would be easily read by almost any device, any decent text editor.

The excuse he had given Jill about malware suddenly struck him as too valid. The IM was, however improbably, a hoax and its attachment harmful to the computers. On the desk, he had several USB drives he often used with the laptop. He inserted two and copied Egg.Timer.ftp.doc to each USB. He removed the drive and set it next to the laptop.

In a hysterical excess of caution, he put one USB drive in his pocket.

It might explode.

Ha, Ha, Leigh.

He truly did not know what to expect from her.

"Oh, brother."

He got out of the chair, took out the pocketed USB drive and parked it under the hallway angel. Since he was conceding to superstition for security, he figured the skirt of an angel made sense.

The integrity of Leigh's laptop was all important. His desktop was just a tool he could repair. Itching to open the file, he took the time to check the status of the desktop's backup external drive. It was current. He had done so little with either computer in the previous week, the backup program had had little to copy.

He disconnected the external drive.

He made a DVD copy of the desktop's Windows 7 operating system.

Good to go.

Expecting almost anything, Julian clicked on the file. Microsoft Word opened and, after a few seconds, displayed what was a text file. The file contained nothing but an ftp location, an ftp directory, username, password and other data for a hosted web account. To be safe, Julian went full analog and jotted the details down by hand. He then opened Notepad. Back in the document, he highlighted the key text and hit control-C to copy it.

Sliding the cursor back to Notepad, he keyed *Paste.*

The desktop crashed.

"Thus, killing the messenger."

Reassured that the laptop had not reacted, he initiated a reboot for the desktop.

Too impatient to sit, waiting, Julian headed for the kitchen, nodding at the storage angel as he strode past. He took the steps so quickly, his feet slipped twice. He deserved to fall but did not.

Genetically granted balance.

Nothing external.

The tablet sat on the kitchen table, snoozing. Julian opened it, and half the screen was dedicated to the suspended egg timer program, stuck on a count of zero. He had opted out of auto-reset in a fit of pique earlier. Julian set it to auto but had to restart it, initially, with *play*. His finger hesitated over the arrow icon. He checked the tablet's automatic time against his manually set watch, microwave, and range top. They were within a minute of each other.

Within the margin of error.

He pressed *play* in the egg timer app. When nothing happened, he tried three more times. The tablet just sat there. It showed no dancing, no music, ticking countdown.

Come on, Leigh. What?

He hit play again.

He finally got a response: The tablet crashed.

After boot, the app did not reappear.

~ ~ ~

Staring at the computer screens did not make the computers comply. Even his faithful desktop had not fully recovered from Egg.Timer.ftp.doc crash. *Downloads* did not display the file. Yet another couple searches failed to find it. The desktop would not complete the copy routine for the file from either USB drive.

Its Egg did not dance, either, but at least the frozen Egg was present. First, the laptop and then the tablet had banished the egg, its timer, and its music.

Julian had begun to think of it as Egg. He was not anthropomorphizing Egg. To him, it was more demon than human. He did not give it a name he could repeat in public. In most of the varying routines, Egg did not lip-sync, but Julian thought of the songs Egg's performances.

Leigh had drawn Egg. She had animated Egg, seemingly, to give the little devil a life of its own. Julian preferred that to Leigh's continuing to control the leggy demon for torture purposes.

She was kidding about that.

Right?

He went to his ftp program and entered the parameters he had hand copied. The ftp directory on the Web would show him Leigh's files and, normally, let him download them. He did not, for one second, believe he would be able to do that.

Once the parameters were set, he hit *Enter*.

Predictably, the connection failed. Then, the desktop crashed.

After unplugging the desktop for thirty seconds, Julian rebooted. He tried a different, much more sophisticated utility to copy Egg.Timer.ftp.doc back onto the desktop. The program was designed to run in its own *sandbox*, a separate part of the system. Once he keyed the copy command, the utility froze but not take the desktop with it.

Progress.

As if to torment him for his pathetic optimism, the desktop crashed.

Julian waited to reboot, as he tried to decide what might work. When he had, the desktop narrowed his options by one. The Father Time icon was missing.

Though the icon had disappeared from the laptop and the tablet, its abrupt departure from the desktop shook him badly. He slumped in his chair. The desktop had been one of his reality anchors. He was running out of anchors.

He lost track of time while he recovered. When he had, he returned to the file manager and the USB drive's list of files. He deleted every file except Egg.Timer.ftp.doc file. The deletion when through without a hitch.

Overly buoyed by that success, he tried to attach the file from the USB drive to an email. The attachment command, all by itself, crashed the desktop.

After another reboot, he highlighted the Egg.Timer file. He right-clicked on the file name, chose *properties* and waited for the crash.

The property window opened benignly and showed the file's author as *Leigh's laptop*. The creation date was a few weeks before Leigh's death. She had not told him about the file, let alone given him a copy. She had intended the ftp account just for her own private use.

"That's not like you."

The next piece of data pierced all the way through Julian's heart. The *Last Modification* date was the date of her death, August 19.

The year was not 2012.

"2013! What the hell?" Julian leaned toward the screen as if clarity might change the reading.

It occurred to him that his copying might have changed the year. Under normal circumstances, routine copying maintained all a file's properties, including the creation and last modification dates.

"But we're a long way from normal–"

He reexamined the properties and gaped.

The year 2013 may have had an explanation. The modify date did not.

The *last modified* date had not arrived.

No one would hack the fucking date!

Julian called Frank and Polly. Polly answered.

“Am I nuts?” he began without preface.

“Nuts? Let me check with Frank.” She turned from the phone, repeated the question and came back on. “Uh. Yep. I’m paraphrasing.”

“Isn't Leigh's one-year anniversary more than a week way?”

Polly hesitated and sounded concerned when she asked, “Is that a serious question?”

“Don't go anywhere,” Julian said, hearing the panic in his voice. He took a breath. “I think Leigh... The three minutes? I don't know. I have two thumbs...” He laughed. “I mean I have two thumbs Drives. There's a new document. It's her. Leigh. It has to be. It can’t be the computers.”

“Julian,” Polly began to say. “What is?”

“All of it.”

~ ~ ~

Frank sat at the table in the Leonards’ breakfast nook. He had a small plate ready for toast. He split his attention between his wife and the toaster. When he heard the word nuts, he focused on Polly and circled his ear with an index finger in response to her question about Julian.

After conveying the gist of his answer, Polly examined the phone before she hung it up. “Can an intelligent man go insane in three minutes?”

“Try repeating them endlessly in your mind,” Frank said. “Give him credit. It has taken a while to get there.”

“Well, it won’t take him long to get here.”

“Don’t let him in, for God’s sake.”

“I have to. He's says he's all thumbs.”

“I'll bet he didn't say that. Exactly.”

"*Exact* does not describe that conversation," she said. "It boiled down to thumbs, and *it's her*."

Frank sighed. "It she coming?"

"He didn't say."

"In that case, don't let *them* in."

Frank glanced at the toaster and walked over to flick it off. He then went into the dining room and returned with an unopened magnum bottle of Grey Goose. He placed the vodka on the counter next to the refrigerator. "I believe a pitcher of your world-class Bloody Mary is in order."

"If this is that serious," Polly said. She cracked open the Grey Goose.

"It is that serious."

He did not return the Grey Goose to the freezer. "You get the toast," he said, "I need my notes from lunch the other day."

"The Erin disaster?" she asked with a sly smile as he passed her.

Frank and Polly had finished their toast and a two-ounce Bloody sampling each before they heard a car in the driveway. Polly went into the dining room to size up their state of their friend.

Julian slammed the car door, not in anger, but because he was rushing, and the laptop made it awkward. He reached the front steps and smiled strangely at Polly inside the open door. "Hi." He tossed something small in the air from his free hand and missed it when it fell. He laughed, as strangely as he had smiled. He picked it up and climbed the three steps to the stoop.

"Good God," she said, with a frown.

"Yeah. I know."

Despite his grizzled state, Polly kissed him on both cheeks. "That burned. And not in a good way."

"I've been preoccupied."

"That's not what Frank called it." She wove her arm inside his. "Come one. Bring your shadows and thumbs into the kitchen."

Julian did not move. He opened his hand and looked at the USB drive.

Polly took the drive and inspected it. "Looks harmless." She then patted the laptop. "Hello, Leigh."

He frowned, then smiled. "I wish that sounded crazy to me."

"You'd better come in."

Frank was brushing some crumbs off his notebook computer with a blue envelope when the entered the kitchen. The Leonard kitchen was twice the size of the Cochran's, with a breakfast nook large enough for a table and four chairs.

"You've gone to seed, even since lunch," Frank said, without getting up.

"You know how I lost those three minutes?" Julian asked.

"Not yet, but I will."

"Good. Because, now, I've lost Egg... the egg, too." He gestured with the laptop.

"Leigh's singing, dancing egg?"

"It doesn't sing, does it?" Polly asked. "I thought it lip-syncs."

"Sometimes and badly," Julian said, his red-rimmed eyes wide. He sat himself and the laptop down diagonally from Frank and his notebook. "But not anymore. Not since this morning."

Frank asked, "Isn't that an improvement?"

"First on this," Julian barreled on. He left the laptop closed. "Then the tablet. Now, it's just gone. On everything."

Over Bloody Mary's, Julian recounted all his efforts for the prior few day, initially in excruciating detail but progressively less so. It sounded, even to him, like compulsive repetition. "I've tried everything. A lot."

Polly handed Frank the USB drive. "He brought Leigh to help."

Julian looked at the couple's dueling expressions. "She's not on the drive. I don't think."

"I meant the laptop."

"What *is* on this thumb drive?" Frank asked, calmly.

"Right now, it's only a *doc* file. Leigh created it."

"When?"

"About... a couple weeks before she died."

"Did she tell you anything about it? At the time?"

"I don't think so. If she did, I don't remember it."

"It's been tough, Julian," Polly said. "Forgetting for a while is good."

"I think I would remember. It's her ftp log-on. Maybe, where everything is. Why would she hide it from me? I knew about the egg app. It wasn't a secret." Julian rocked a bit. "I guess... We didn't expect it. Not that day, for sure. Maybe, she just didn't get around to giving me a copy."

"But now she has?"

Frank shook his head. "I doubt that."

"That's partly true," Julian said. "Only she didn't. Jill did."

Polly and Frank exchanged looks of confusion.

"How does Jill come in?" Polly asked.

"This morning," Julian explained, "Jill said I... Leigh's laptop sent it to her in an IM. At 4:22 this morning." He grew more intense. "But I was using it at 4:22."

Polly laughed. "How about 4:19?"

"Pretty much constantly from 2:00 through 5:00. The IM was never inactive," Julian said. He held up a hand to stop a question from Frank. "Don't worry. I checked the logs, too. More than once. I do everything more than once. There was

Nothing. No activity, not until Jill IM'ed me. On my account. It has never been set up on the laptop. It was Leigh's."

"You're sure."

"There hasn't been any IM activity on Leigh's laptop since a year ago. You want to check the logs, yourself?" Julian inched the laptop toward Frank but kept his hand firmly on its lid.

"Of course not," Frank said, his tone reassuring. "Jesus. It's not that I believe you're–"

"What? That I've imagined all this. I've lied to you?"

"I've seen the laptop's time glitch," Frank replied, evenly. "I've seen the egg timer. Those are real." Frank signaled Polly to intercede.

"What's in it?" she asked, her hand on Julian's shoulder, "The document from this morning."

Suddenly, the rigidity left Julian. "I can't access it anymore. But I made notes before that happened." He pulled the wrinkled yellow note page from his pocket and started to hand it to Polly.

"No wonder no one uses *sheets* of paper anymore. They're longer but aren't *stiff* enough," she said.

"I'm sorry..." Julian followed Polly's eyes and saw Frank's scrawled blue-envelope notes. "I'm just a three-minute kinda guy."

Frank said, "The solicitation was addressed to *current resident*." He smiled. "It's not like they *know* me. Right Polly?"

Julian and Polly laughed, blowing out much of the tension.

"Of course, dear."

Julian held out his notes to Polly. "I kind of buried the lead."

"No more innuendo, please."

"You'll see." He handed her the paper.

Polly looked it over. She shrugged. "I don't see anything. The ftp log-in info. You talked about that."

Frank took it from her and gave it a quick once over. "That's all it said?"

"Take another look." Julian become quite calm, despite his anticipation. "The dates."

Frank studied the paper. He looked up at Julian, surprised. "The creases made it hard to see." He handed it back to Polly.

"Okay. What did I miss?"

"The date last modified, Pol," Frank said.

Polly's large eyes grew even bigger. "Uh oh."

"Yeah." Julian felt relieved. He had not imagined it. "Uh oh."

"We've gone from three minutes eggs to more than a week… of what?"

Frank moved his notebook aside and went to move Leigh's laptop in front of him.

Julian slapped his hand on the laptop. "What are you doing?"

"I thought I'd try–"

"Don't." Julian pulled the laptop back in front of him. "I'm sorry. I'm just so afraid…" He grimaced. "I was afraid to take it to Renegades. It hasn't been the same since. I shouldn't have brought it, now. I wasn't thinking. I just grabbed it."

"Thinking what?" Polly asked gently before Frank could comment.

"She might get mad enough to erase everything."

"She's not like that," Polly objected. "I mean *really*. It's Leigh we're talking about."

Frank kept quiet for a moment. "What else is there? The egg timer app is gone. You've looked for it. You have the ftp log-in information. There's nothing to lose, is there?"

"That's just it. I don't know."

"All right. Let's assume it is – and I don't – Polly is right. Leigh wants..." Frank threw up his hands. "I can't believe I'm saying this, but Leigh is using the laptop for something. Erasing it would be counterproductive."

"I suppose."

"Okay. The ftp. Did try to log on? Onto the ftp site?"

He nodded. "It didn't work. It's like..."

"She doesn't want you to?" Polly finished.

"It just seemed safer to bring it here," Julian said, abashed. "It's like a second home?"

"Oh, thanks, Julian," Polly said, with a grin. "We can give out haunted thumb drives on Halloween."

"I meant that you know, the house," Julian explained. "Maybe, she... it is tied to the house. Less... attentive?"

"Another reason to run the laptop here."

"He's right, Julian," Polly agreed. She took Julian's hand off the laptop and opened the lid.

The laptop began to awaken. The three of them watched as the screen appeared, with no suggestion of the egg timer app.

"Where's your ftp program?

"The Start menu."

Frank ran the ftp access program. He read the details from the notepad and entered the login and directory information. "Okay. Do you want me to continue or would you rather?"

"I've tried. Time for a change."

None of them expected the procedure to work.

It did.

"Son of a bitch," Julian said.

"Nice, Frank."

On the local directory side, there were no files listed. The internet side of the ftp host window showed only two files.

"This isn't her only site," Frank said. "There are no music files or graphic files."

The files time and date properties were listed:

File Name Lilys.List.xls
Created 06/14/12 @ 16:13:44
Last Mod 08/19/13 @ 22:11:25

File Name Index.Egg.xap
Created 04/02/12 @ 11:18:02
Last Mod 08/19/13 @ 08:12:00

File Name Video.Me.mp4
Created 08/19/12 @ 22:09:00
Last Mod 08/19/13 @ 22:12:00

"How can that be?" Frank asked, purely rhetorically. "Someone is fucking with us."

"Could someone change those dates?"

"Sure, but why? Who would care? Besides, it might cause execution problems." He went to strike a key and Julian stopped him. "What?"

"Don't log out. This may be our only chance."

"Maybe we only get one look," Polly said. "And what's an *xap* file?"

"It's a Windows app file, presumably for the egg-timer," Frank said. "Don't worry, I'm just going up a level. It's safe. I'm not logging out."

"Okay."

Frank jumped a directory level on the web side. "One more." He clicked again. "There it is."

"I'm afraid to look," Polly said, her hands over her eyes.

"Me, too. What is it, Frank?"

"This last access date is harder to fake," he explained. "Nobody thinks of it."

It was August 19, 2012, 22:15:00.

"Shit," Julian said. "That's last year. And the files are in the future."

"So, this is all fucked up?" Polly asked. "I mean, right?"

Frank returned to Leigh's ftp directory. The screen flickered but stabilized.

"That was close," Julian said.

"Let me download those programs," Frank said. "At least, if it will let me..."

Julian grimace. "I don't know."

Polly said, "If Leigh will let you."

"It's the internet, guys."

"The *cloud*," she said, waving her fingers.

"Jillian?" he asked. "Your call."

Julian kept his eyes on the screen for a long time. "It seems so risky. I think... I want it... To be true."

"Of course, you do," Polly said. "Me, too."

"Your premise is that it's Leigh. She's the nicest person I've ever met."

"True," Polly said. "But something's not right. I can feel it. Don't do it."

"Yes. I think we have to," Julian said, his voice firming. "Give the download a try."

Frank highlighted the files as a block. All he had to do was press *Control* and drag them across from the web side to the local side of the ftp window. "Here we go."

He slowly dragged the three files and tried to deposit them in the local directory. Nothing happened. "Okay. Let's try one at a time." He highlighted the first file and dragged it.

The transfer seemed to take forever. The copy finally stuck.

"Well," Julian said.

Polly breathed out. "It does not feel like champagne, yet."

"And you're our optimist."

Frank targeted file two, the smallest of the three. After it had planted itself, he eyed the third file. "This one is an MP4. It's much bigger."

Julian shrugged, and Frank went ahead.

It took almost forty seconds of silent waiting, the MP4 file landed.

In the next instant, all three files disappeared from both sides of the window. There was nothing but blank space.

"Fuck," Frank said.

The laptop crashed.

Frank pressed palms against his temples and left them there.

"Boom," Julian said, with a post-tension laugh.

"You don't believe me," Polly said, "but I could feel it."

"So," Julian said, bordering on pleased. "Now, she's temperamental?" He rebooted the laptop.

The three of them did not move or speak during the reboot. Frank's faith in the absence of faith was shaken. Polly hoped Leigh's triumph would inspire, even salvage, Julian.

Julian watched the laptop as it went through its startup. It looked fine, with its normal icons and without the egg timer app. The clock was three minutes behind.

Polly noticed the time, too. "Wow. There it is. Three minutes."

Julian started and turned his attention to the three files on paper. He had skimmed over one. One made no sense to him on two levels.

"An MP4 file. A video," Julian said, to himself. He repeated louder, "It's a video. Why does she have this video up there?"

"Why not?" Polly asked. "It's not unusual for people when they are sick. You know..." She did not complete the *leaving a message* thought. "Leigh was in advertising."

"She stayed away from the video side. She never did more than the sets for filming ads."

Frank said, "Everyone does video these days."

"Not us. But she had three files on the ftp and one's that video. When? She had put all her time into the Egg app. I don't see how she'd have time for a video, let alone the inclination."

"We know she uploaded that one," Frank said.

"It's news to me. Up to know, I only knew she was working on the Egg. And on Lily's List–"

"Which is?" Polly asked. "And an index of cat photos?"

Julian slowly shook his head.

"Well?"

"She called it that because it was her *recipe* – that's what she called it – for a death as peaceful as Lily's was."

"Oh. That list."

It took them a few seconds to recover from that explanation.

Julian spoke first. "As for the video, she'd never done a video in her life. She had never even used the damned camera before that night," Julian said, baffled. "I mean, literally, she had never used it. She was playing with it for the first time... before I... Like two minutes before I left. It's too weird."

Polly hugged Julian's shoulders. "It's all too weird, Julian."

Frank rose. "Hold on a minute. I have my old laptop. It's about the same age as Leigh's. I want to try something." He hurried out of the Kitchen.

"He never throws his toys away." Polly poured herself a few ounces of Bloody Mary. She held up the pitcher as an offer.

He moved his glass into position. "I think I'd better. This is too hard sober. Besides, these are too good to pass up."

"She's not trying to hurt you. You know that."

Julian nodded. "Then what? What do you feel?"

"I don't know. I just feel something is off."

Frank returned with a laptop and a cable with a small card attached to each end. "It's vintage Windows 7." He indicated the cable/cards combination. "I used this Express Card rig to transfer my data this notebook last year. It's faster than USB. Then, aside from a couple programs, including the transfer program, I wiped the drive last year after I got the notebook, in case I wanted to give it away."

"Which, history teaches, would never happen."

"As usual," Frank countered, "it was worthwhile I did not."

After he had refused to elaborate, Polly and Julian refused to ask him to do so.

Polly broke first. "Okay. You told us that long story for a reason. Don't leave us hanging."

"If Julian approves," Frank said, "I want to use that program to clone Leigh's laptop."

The plan brought a stunned silence.

"After what just happened?" she demanded. "Are you–" Polly cut herself off, closed her eyes and put her head back.

"Jesus, Frank," Julian said. "I don't know."

"We got to see the ftp directory."

Polly leveled her eyes at Julian and took a deep breath. "I think you should do it."

"Meaning?"

"It's not like the download, somehow," she said. "It doesn't matter. I think it's okay."

"A feeling, again."

"Not really. I don't know. I just think... It seems to me those files are much more important, especially the video file. Cloning probably doesn't matter right now."

"You do have the best instincts," Frank said.

"I think Polly's right. Those files are the important ones, and they are not on the laptop." Julian stopped thinking about it. "Go ahead, Frank."

Frank plugged the Express Cards into each laptops' slot and went into the cloning program. "The hard disks are the same size, so our first hurdle is getting Leigh's to accept to the program. It runs on a Linux kernel, so the Windows system will be cloned, too."

"If you say so, dear."

"We'll know in about a minute."

"We have to remember to breathe," Polly advised, pouring some more Bloody Mary for herself and Julian. "For our oxygen deprivation. This stuff has more oxygen atoms than water."

"That's the best rationale for Chem 101, I've ever heard," Frank said. He finished the pitcher. "You realize it's still early."

"It's lunch time somewhere."

Frank held up his hand. "That was quick. We're ready to start. Still want to do it, Julian?"

"Yep. If it works, it works," Julian said. "The files will still be on the ftp site. Still in the Cloud. Even if we won't have them, she will."

Frank initialized the routine. A black and white transfer window opened and showed file names whizzing by and a percentage of files transferred. "So far so good, but don't watch. It will take more time." He turned both screens away from view.

Julian said, "And it's bad luck."

They all laughed.

Frank glanced at the clone's screen. "Still going."

"Whew."

"Do I have time to make some grilled cheese? Polly asked. "I'm getting bloody tipsy."

"I'm sure you do, Pol. We're at twenty-one percent. This will take some time."

"I'd help," Julian said, "but... Do you have a fire extinguisher?"

~ ~ ~

The transfer continued without a hitch, reaching ninety-seven percent by the time Polly presented two piles, one of halved, crusty grilled cheese sandwiches, the other napkins. She was a master of the grilled cheese sandwich, but their surfaces had a sheen of butter.

Frank took one, looked at his fingers and put it back. He used a napkin. "I'll have to wait, damn it. We don't want my fingers sliding to the *Explode* key by mistake. We only have a couple minutes left."

"Do we know what key that is?" Julian asked.

"*Enter* has worked so far."

Polly and Julian three half sandwiches.

"Damn, this is good, Polly. Thank you."

"Thanks, but you aren't much of a food critic these days, Mr. Pizza."

"Yeah, but I know cheese when–"

"Done!" Frank spun the clone and the laptop toward them. Both screens said, *transfer complete."*

"What happens–" Julian had not finished his question when Frank turned off both laptops. "Uh, next."

Frank reached for a grilled cheese. "I don't know about you, but I eat." He took a sizable bite and smiled at Polly. "If I didn't marry you for your grilled cheese, I was a fool."

"No need to boast, dear."

The laptops disks whirred quietly, but the sound was lost for the chewing. Finally, the *Windows* logo appeared. They stopped eating. Frank wiped his hands. He took out his smartphone.

"Hard hats anyone?" Polly covered her eyes with her fingers. She peeked out through two of them.

Julian pulled one of her arms down, with little effort. "I think we are relatively safe."

"Oh, that's reassuring."

"I think you two decide Leigh wouldn't hurt you," Frank said, "Physically."

"We're not very reliable, Julian and I."

The laptop screens filled in with identical icons. Neither showed the Father Time icon. The time display was an exact match.

Frank checked the time on his phone and showed it to Polly and Julian.

Polly looked at both computers. "You did it, Frank!"

"We should try the ftp," Julian suggested. "On the clone."

After another wipe of his fingers, Frank called up the ftp program on the cloned laptop. Leigh's laptop showed no activity.

"Why don't they both show the same thing," Polly asked.

"It's not a mirror or a screencast. This is essentially the same machine from the operating system up."

"But it's not the same."

"No, Julian. Not quite. It is as close as we can get without having the exact same model."

Once the clone's ftp columns appeared, Frank ran the same program on Leigh's laptop. The display was the same. "I'm going to run them one at a time since they will use the same username and password. One connection may lock out the other. There's no need to add that variable."

Frank clicked on Leigh's *Connect* first.

"Any reason you picked Leigh's first?" Julian asked. "We have to see that one."

"Not really. Just a baseline."

Leigh's laptop showed the two empty columns.

Julian did not express his disappointment. He had hoped Leigh's laptop would again show that the ftp site on the internet would have the files, especially the video file. He just wanted to see them, to know they were there for some future access.

"Well, she didn't put anything back," Polly said.

Frank logged out and connected on the clone. The columns were equally empty. "Shall we try the USB drive."

Julian shook his head. "I don't want to press our luck. For now. The USB doesn't really matter, anymore. Just those three ftp files."

"I shouldn't have tried to move all three," Frank said. "The first two seemed to have worked. Maybe, the video file was too big."

"Or maybe," Polly said, "it wasn't time to get the video."

"Not time." Julian leaned back and stretched. "Time. It's all–" He grabbed the wrinkled paper and nodded. "These file dates make no sense, right? I mean it's the *year* that doesn't."

"Oh," Polly said. "But the day and time?"

"The time does make sense." Julian could feel the awareness part the cloud of fatigue. "If the time is correct, Leigh started making the video after I went downstairs." He pulled the paper to smooth the wrinkles when hit finally came to him. "It's three minutes. It's three minutes long! Look." He showed them the paper, pointing to the video file times. "The video! It's of those three minutes!" He looked from one to the other, excitement in his eyes.

"Meaning what?" Frank asked.

"Meaning I can see them!" Julian took a deep breath to counter the excitement of certainty. He could not remember when he last felt that way. "The three minutes. I can see them."

"Oh, Julian." Polly's hand covered her mouth.

Frank steepled his fingers around his nose. "I don't think you want to do that."

"Yes, I have to. *That* is what this about. Don't you see? The video. That's the message."

"But you can't retrieve it," Frank reminded him."

"I think I can," Julian said, calmly. "It's just not time."

"For?"

"For Leigh's message."

Chapter Sixteen

August 19, 2012 10:08:50 PM

As Maroon 5 wound down, Leigh glanced at the Egg timer. Julian would be taking the eggs out in a few seconds. She wanted him to stop, to come back upstairs.

She took several deep breaths to regain control. She pulled herself into a better position. That little movement brought a grimace of pain and a cough.

Leigh picked up three tissues, as a precaution. One tissue would soak through too easily.

She focused on her face and did nothing until she could manage a convincing smile.

It looked so wrong.

Just her.

For irony's sake, she thought, she should time her video message to the egg timer. More than likely, she would delete the video and work on better versions later. The image may have seemed wrong, but that timing would be right.

My time is *counting down.*

Leigh could feel her internal timer counting down. Whatever she wanted to say, she had to say it.

"Ding! Oh, Julian."

It was exactly 10:09 PM when she hit the record button, as Elvis's *Can't Help Falling* began. She spoke into the camera, her weak, raspy voice slightly above a whisper. She did not want Julian to hear. She wanted it to be a surprise.

It is to me!

"You know, Julian, you may never see this video."

She heard Julian call out from the kitchen, "I've got 'em!"

As loudly as she could - not very - she called back exactly the opposite of what she felt. "You have under three–" The character of the cough startled her. She caught it with the tissues, and there was no blood, for a change. Still, it sounded full of fluid. Then, she addressed the camera. "I'm not showing off my new expertise, I'm more practicing–" She smothered the cough with tissue.

The stain was very dark red, almost black. She refused to focus on it and cast the tissues aside, replacing them with a fresh threesome

"Or not," she continued, "I'd better just say it. I can delete it later."

She lacked the breath to say it. She lacked the will to say it. She tried to take a deep breath but should have known better. She coughed again, with the same result. She refreshed the tissue.

"This my first attempt at a last video for you–"

The crash in energy came suddenly. Her head dropped, and her hands fell off her lap. She recovered but not all the way, not even close.

"Don't be disappointed in me." She continued, halting for a cough. She raised her voice. She had to be louder than the song. "It's because I love you too much."

It seemed to take forever, even longer than it took to realize the truth of it.

She believed that the time was as fitting as her message. As time counted down, as she said the unexpected words, Leigh felt so much lighter.

~ ~ ~

Julian took the two eggs from their icy bowl and put them onto a flat plate. There, he chopped them to a small enough size, but not too small. Some of the yokes bled over the white. There was none of the *yuk* of underdone eggs that nauseated him.

She was right about the three minutes. "You guys are perfect."

He dried the bowl and slid the pieces of egg into it. Once upon a time, Leigh had prepared soft-boiled eggs in egg cups. Ultimately, she decided chopping made for better distribution of the butter, pepper, and salt. Her final tweak was the use of Sea Salt only.

He had stopped adding more than a hint of pepper because it made her cough.

Julian dropped the butter on the floor. He glared at it, as Elvis sang a chorus. He had other sticks in the freezer, but he needed the softer butter squashed on the floor. He let it sit there.

He finished removing the shells of the eggs.

Such a bad design, egg shells.

Dancing or not.

He got a spatula from the utensil drawer and scooped up enough of the butter, trying to scoop only the upper half.

"You'll never know," he whispered, looking at the ceiling. He smeared some butter onto the eggs.

The tablet's egg timer's clock, an unforgiving taskmaster. He had to pick up the pace.

He sprinkled the Sea Salt and a whisper of pepper. He put the bowl on the tray, followed by the fork and teaspoon. Leigh thought soups spoons were just for soup.

Are there egg spoons?

He admired his handiwork for a couple heartbeats. He could feel them – proving how nerve-wracking timeliness could be – and double-checked that he had everything. It would defeat the purpose if he arrived on time with an incomplete tray.

Julian grabbed the tray and checked the tablet before strode out the kitchen.

Not fast enough.

Elvis was almost done. He dangerously took two steps at a time. He could hear Elvis go into his last, drawn-out "... with you." A backup choir came up along with a piano.

"Julian," Leigh said, her voice almost inaudible.

He was a little annoyed. "I'm almost there, for Christ's sake," He said, landing on the hallway.

The piano hit its penultimate note.

Julian planted his elbow on the door to clear the tray.

The piano hit its ultimate, low note.

"Ding!" the voice said, indifferent to artistry.

"Oh, for God's sake."

The door swung the rest of the way.

"Oh, Julian."

Julian dropped the tray about the same time the laptop hit the floor.

"Oh, fuck, no! Leigh! You can't–"

In his mind, Julian rushed to take her left hand as it reached towards him, squeezed it and woke her up. In reality, he did not move at all. The hand that reached for him was her right, far, far away.

"God damn it, Leigh! I was right here."

Things did happen in the next three minutes and the gulps of time beyond, but Julian remembered none of them accurately. He depended on Frank and Polly to keep it all straight.

Chapter Seventeen

August 18, 2013

Whatever the dream, Julian had slept through it, his head on his chest, tears still on his cheeks.

The desktop egg timer ran, softly playing Maroon 5's *Give a Little More.*

The laptop's screen showed its own desktop with a few icons sprinkled about, but not so much of a *scythe* or anything else of interest.

Julian woke with a start, the start being apt. It took him a while. He could not decide if the popping open of the IM window or its faint tone did the trick. As his eyes focused, he could see it was Jill.

Who else would it be?

> *JIL – What's new?*
> *JUL – Jesus, I have to get more sleep.*

He checked the laptop's screen. Finding nothing. He imagined it all. He went back to the IM.

> *JUL – Nothing. And I mean nothing*
> *JIL – How's the 3 minute thing?*
> *JIL – Did Frank sweet talk it into parity?*
> *JIL – He can be so charming. Not.*
> *JUL –Oh. I guess there is something*

JIL – Give.
JUL – It's complicated.
JIL – I hate that phrase.
JIL – It means someone's lying with me.
JUL – Summary: She got pissed and crashed on him, too.
JIL – She? You're a believer?
JUL – It would be romantic, don't you think?
JIL – You know I do.
JUL – Then Frank cloned the laptop.
JIL – Cloned? How?
JUL – That's the complicated part.
JIL – Never mind, then.
JUL – The uncomplicated part?
JUL – It lost three minutes, too.
JIL – No shit?
JUL – Shovels full.
JIL – I'll bet Frank's still a holdout.

Julian looked away from the laptop, composing a reply. Frank's response was also complicated. He still had the strongest dose of denial. Julian knew Frank, on and on, suspected that an unknown clone of Julian – Frank often referred to Old Julian, New Julian, and Interim Julian – had concocted the whole thing, the files, the strange dates in ftp directory, some sort of computer-crashing virus.

It would be simpler.

But not as romantic.

When his eyes returned to the laptop screen, he saw an icon slowly appear below the IM window. It was, distinctly, a curled up, very blond cat. The text below the icon read, *Lily's List.*

"No... fucking... way." Julian rocked forward and studied the icon. It was tiny, but he recognized the image. It was pulled from a photo of Lily, one he had scanned himself a few weeks earlier.

Don't tell Frank!

He checked the desktop. There was no Lily icon. The tablet showed nothing new, either. He looked at his phone with the same non-result.

JIL – *Julian?*
JUL – *She sent me something else.*
JIL – *What? Leigh did?*
JUL – *It's a file, with an icon of a curled cat.*
JUL – *Guess the color.*
JIL – *What do you mean?*
JUL – *It's blond. The icon.*
JIL – *So, it's from Leigh?*
JUL – *It is a picture of Lily. I recognize it.*
JIL – *Oh. My. God. You're sure?*
JUL – *Absolutely.*
JUL – *Lily's List. That's its name.*
JUL – *It's also one of the file names on Leigh's ftp site.*
JIL – *Leigh had an ftp site?*
JUL – *Yep. All of three files.*

Julian almost told Jill about the video file. He knew it was too soon.

JUL – *When Frank tried to download them, boom.*
JUL – *All three vanished.*
JUL – *And Leigh's laptop crashed.*
JUL – *But, now, today, one of them shows up with Lily?*
JIL – *Let me check mine.*

Julian waited for a few seconds, trying to separate out his emotions: Fear, hope, some anger. He even remained a little pissed at Frank for thinking him a fraud... not a fraud, just a psychological puddle of goo. Frank knew him well enough to know the latter. Looking at himself objectively, he would have gone with goo, too. It had occurred to him, more than once.

JIL – *I have nothing. Even the file I sent you is gone.*
JUL – *When:*
JIL – *I tried to delete it, but couldn't.*
JIL – *I didn't pay attention after that.*
JIL – *It's not there.*
JUL – *I have to call Frank.*

Julian's cell phone rang. He knew who was calling before the second ring. The caller ID confirmed it: *Frank's Skype.*

"You have it, too," Julian stated.

"Meow," Polly said, with a hollow, distant, speaker sound.

"I heard that. Barely."

"We're on the notebook's Skype. Its mic sucks."

"Why don't you stop pacing," Frank suggested. "Julian, any ideas?"

"You *are* kidding," Julian said, blandly. "I'm IM'ing Jill. Let me tell her to hold on."

JUL – *Guess whose clone just got the same thing.*
JIL – *This is getting scary.*
JUL – *Stand by. Let me talk to them.*
JIL – *I'm afraid to log off, now.*
JIL – *Oh, and, hi, Leigh.*

Julian held his phone to his ear as if he did not want anyone else to hear, as if Jill could hear him.

No. As if she *can.*

But she can.

He decided to stay off the speaker anyway, to avoid the dual tunnel effect.

"Okay, Frank."

"It suddenly appeared–"

"Nice kitty touch, Leigh," Polly added, her voice clearer.

"I agree, Polly. I know that picture of Lily. We've all seen it."

After a brief pause, Polly moaned. "I know it was that ham's favorite pose. But you mean that picture?"

"What do you mean?" Frank asked. "That picture?"

Polly answered. "The icon, silly. It's a picture of Lily. I think it was one of Leigh's favorites."

"When she took it, she called it the *definitive Lily*."

"Boy, is she making a point," Polly said.

"Have you opened it, Julian?"

"Hell, no. I'm afraid just to look at it."

"Should we come over? Should we, Frank?"

Julian steadied himself. He could not relieve the tension, but he could try thinking clearly. "Let's just opened the God damned thing. It's probably just a file we get to see, finally."

"It's the right time, Frank. We can open it."

"It's here. Whoever sent it. It's here."

"I'm starting to believe you," Frank added. "Let me try."

"Welcome to the fold, dear."

"Not quite, yet, thanks."

"Hang on a sec." Julian wondered how cloned could a clone be. It might not work and screw up everything. He had an idea, one that made no sense, but seemed appropriate.

"Frank. We're clones, right? Let's clone the action. Do it at the same time. Make her crash us both, if she wants to be difficult."

Frank positioned the cursor over the Lily icon. "I'm ready if you are."

Julian did the same. He took a breath. "Ready."

"Ready."

"Go."

The laptop's screen opened a Microsoft Excel window and displayed a new version, one with large, merged cells for text he had never seen before. The entire block of cells with words or figures had s a very light gray background. There were a couple single-cell exceptions. Expecting a crash, Julian was speechless.

"Do you have it, Julian?" Frank asked, excited.

Frank excited?

"Julian?" Polly joined in.

Julian waited several loud heartbeats for it to crash.

It did not.

What the–

"It never had color… I have never seen any wording before. Honest to God," he said, studying it. It was headed *Lily Recipe*. Leigh had incorporated quite a bit of text into the spreadsheet file. The table had fewer rows and only one dosage column. Atop the dosage table was a row, all in gray, except for two variables, both of those cells were in a blue that almost matched the color of her eyes. The gray cells to the left of the blue cells contained labels: *Weight* and *Tolerance*. The weight variable was set at a sad 91 pounds. The tolerance at 3.

By chance, Julian had the cursor on one of the dosage cells. Without thinking, he clicked. Nothing happened.

Just as well.

Oh, the cell is protected.

He moved the cursor from one gray-shaded cell to another and dared to click on them. Nothing happened, no crash and no ability to affect the cell in any way. He clicked on the lower text cell, with the same lack of effect. He tried the blue *weight* cell. It allowed him to change the number.

All the dosage cells changed. Only the variable cells were subject to editing.

Smart, girl.

He changed the weight back to 91, to be safe.

Leigh had written up text paragraphs of more detailed instructions below the table, including the proper order and timing of dosages. He had never seen those instructions. "It is much more refined." The word sounded bizarre in the context.

Frank and Polly leaned back and looked at each other. They had never seen Leigh's spreadsheet, but Julian had described it, generally. What they were seeing was far more elaborate than his description. He had never mentioned any text at all.

At the top of the document was a centered note to Julian.

Dearest Julian,
I hope to do this myself,
but if you are stuck following my Lily List,
I'm so, so sorry.
I know how hard it will be for you.
But it is important.
I am getting very weak.
Don't forget to enter my real weight.
Dosage is critical.
I have set my tolerance level to 3.
That should work.

PS: I'm am making a video as I do this.
To tell you something that I just decided.
Something I can't bring myself to say
out loud to you or even to write down.
I am a little ashamed, but I know I am right.

Love, eternally (And I will prove it)

Leigh

"Jesus. What is she talking about?"

"Ashamed?" Polly asked, her voice shaky. "Leigh? That's crazy."

Hang on, guys. Let me get back to Jill." He put his phone on speaker so that he could type a message to Jill and stay on with Frank and Polly.

JUL *– It opened.*
JIL *– Really?*
JUL *– It is Lily's List. Leigh's suicide directions.*
JUL *– I've never seen this one.*
JIL *– Pardon the French but WTF?*

Polly listened to Julian type and muted the microphone on the Notebook. "My God. Poor Julian."

"Maybe, she's just ashamed of being scared," Frank said.

"Maybe. I hadn't thought of that." Polly reread the text. "It doesn't sound like that. It's something she suddenly decided. Fright is an emotion. Maybe, you can decide an emotion. No one else can."

"I hope this is the last of it."

Polly stoked the back of Frank's head. "It's not," she said. "You know better than that."

"Know *what* better?"

"This is the beginning."

"Of?"

She had no simple answer. The one she had was woefully incomplete. "Of whatever she wants it to be."

JIL *– Hello. Again. WTF?*

JUL – *It's different. It has directions.*
JUL – *And I think she has the dosages linked to her body weight, as a variable.*
JIL – *Why?*
JUL – *Her weight went up and down. It would affect the dosages.*
JUL – *She needed the lowest she could risk.*
JUL – *The Vicodin would make her throw up.*
JUL – *The Valium etc. would make her drowsy or affect her will.*
JUL – *She left me a strange note, too. I'll paste it.*
JUL – *If she'll let me.*

Julian highlighted the text of Leigh's note to him, pasted it into a Notepad file and attached it to his next IM entry.

JUL – *Leigh approved. It is attached.*

Jill did not reply for a moment.

"Hey, Frank?"

Frank had to hesitate. Polly was sobbing too loudly. She nodded, and he keyed off the mute. "Yes?"

"What do you think about trying to find the video again? It seems like Leigh is lightening up on us."

"I wish you'd stop doing that."

"Being incurably optimistic."

"Attributing every except the weather to Leigh. It's unnerving."

Polly shook her head, and mouthed *don't.*

"Sorry. I'm just so… bewildered."

Polly nodded approval.

"I don't know Julian. About the video," Frank said. "Maybe, we should let good enough be good enough for today."

"I could paste the not in my IM with Jill. We're on a roll. I can feel it."

"Me, too," Polly agreed.

"Okay," Frank said. "Both machines?"

"We haven't rolled that far. Just try it with the clone."

"I think it will crash, Julian."

"Let it. We have to try."

"Okay. Let me try my notebook first. I set up the log-in, but haven't tried it. We will lose the Skype if we crash. If we do, Pol will call you on her cell."

"Fine. I'm going back to Jill."

JUL – *We're going to try finding the video file.*
JIL – *That's some note she wrote you.*
JIL – *I've been crying too much to type.*
JUL – *Hang in there.*
JIL – *You, too.*
JUL – *I'll report back.*

As Julian had IM'ed, Frank had called up both his notebook's and the clone's ftp programs. He logged into the notebook version. He navigated to Leigh's ftp directory. There was nothing there, at all.

"Bupkis on my notebook. But no crash. Here goes the clone."

In the clone's ftp program, Frank hit *Connect.*

The three-file list was back on the web-side column. Lily's List and Egg.Timer.ftp.doc were now on the local panel, as well. Only Video.me.mp4 remained on the right, web, side.

"Shit."

"What?" Polly asked. She followed his finger. "Oh. That's weird."

Frank gave her a look.

"I mean, weird, too."

Frank plugged in a USB drive and copied the Lily List file. He and Polly held their breath. The file simply refused to move, but the clone did not crash.

"I tried to copy Lily's List to a USB, first Julian. No dice."

"But no crash," Polly added. "She's playing nice."

"That's half encouraging."

"I'll try to copy the video file to the local directory."

"Okay."

Frank highlighted the video file and dragged it to the local file. It didn't move. He tried again. The clone crashed.

"Kaboom," Polly said.

"Crash?"

"Yes," Frank said. "First it wouldn't move. I guess that was a warning."

"Believe it or not, the laptop here didn't care," Julian said, too soon. "Oh, fuck. Kaboom, part deux."

~ ~ ~

Frank and Polly had joined Julian on his porch at first, but their voices carried to well. They retreated to the small kitchen.

Julian had his smartphone out, and it continued to run the Egg app, muted.

Polly and Julian sat at the table, sharing space with the laptop, with its version of Lily's List displayed. Frank paced in front of them, Jack Daniels in hand. Since he had not been to Julian's recently enough to check the inventory, Frank had brought his own. It proved unnecessary, but, given what he had seen lately, the idea of a backup appealed to him.

Julian poured a frosty Grey Goose for Polly and one for himself. He had a pair of Valiums still in his hand. Polly had already borrowed one. Unlike Frank, she traveled light.

The cloned laptop sat on the counter, next to the TV.

Jill had joined the *kitchen cabinet*, by phone, voice-only Skype on her cell. To be safe, the call was connected via Polly's iPhone speaker.

Jill had floated to Julian the idea of a video conference.

"With these laptops?"

"Oh."

To ease everyone's anxiety, Jill and Frank kicked up their usual relationship.

"Wine? You're not serious, Jill," Frank explained, after sipping more *Jack*. "This is not the occasion for twenty-four proof."

Jill did not believe Frank was actually an *asshole*, but she kept that to herself.

In her own kitchen, Jill poured off the last ounces of a Chardonnay. She went to her fridge and pulled out another brand. "My next bottle of wine is a mellow *organic*. Take that, Frank."

"Where do you even find something like that?"

"Try the not-sour-mash aisle."

"Frank would get lost," Polly said.

Julian watched the Valium jittering in his hand. He took put them out of their misery with a Grey Goose chaser. "So. Aside from organic wine, we can't find the MP4 file anywhere but the ftp aisle."

"And we can't move it or play it."

"Yes, Frank, but we locals at least *can* stare at it," Polly said. "Sorry, Jill."

For a moment, all four remained silent.

Jill finally spoke. "I think you guys are right. It's not time."

"I've abstained," Frank insisted.

"I don't think you can do that," Jill said. "Take a risk."

"I'm here, talking to you, aren't I?"

"That hurt." Jill laughed.

"Sorry, Jill. I'm frustrated. I'm out of my depth... Or height? I don't know. This is your territory, not mine."

Polly said, "That would be pretending. This is beyond all of us."

"It comes down to *we wait for her,*" Jill said. "Call me if anything happens. Whenever it happens. Good night, lady and gentlemen. Oh, Frank, you, too."

"It's nice to be remembered."

"No problem. Sleep in shifts. Bye."

"Wouldn't that be nice. Sleep, I mean," Polly said. "Waiting is all we've got."

Frank shrugged and drank. "We can drink in shifts."

"Okay." Polly sipped very little Grey Goose. "Julian. Your shift."

He sighed as some vodka put him at the back of the queue. "Why? Why this way? The *way* it's happening has to mean something."

"I agree," Polly said.

"They're computer files, for shit's sake, right? Just files?" Frank's nerves were both saturated and frayed. "But what can they mean?"

"Obviously," Julian began. "We've given this a lot of thought. I'll admit, my thinking is not what I'm used, either. But I've kinda gotten used to it. I can't answer your question, Frank," he added, "but I do know two things. For certain."

Polly looked at the table top.

"Go on. I'll take one."

"One: it's coming tomorrow."

"Two: It'll take three minutes." Polly did not look up.

"If there is a third," Julian said, "it might be a certain beautiful, angelic face."

"Or, maybe not," Polly said, meeting his eyes. She shuddered. "We haven't talked about that."

Julian narrowed his eyes. "No, we haven't. Because it doesn't matter. I'll be there..." He did not complete with the *this time* that haunted him.

Frank assured him, "We'll be there with you."

Julian had already considered how it would go. "I don't mean to be melodramatic–a"

"Which usually," Polly interjected, "is a preface to *incredibly stupid.*"

"It's not a group thing, guys."

"There it is.

"Sorry."

"You can't, Julian," Polly pleaded. "You can't be alone."

"It's about those three minutes, Polly," Julian explained, his tone calmed by the Triple V. "It was the two of us. You know I'm right."

Polly was violently shaking her head. "No, no, no."

Frank moved a few feet to put his hand on her shoulder. "Polly is right, but it's your call. You've had to live that three minutes for a year. You can't do it forever."

"Please, Julian." Polly's eyes were big and tearing. "You can't be alone. It might be dangerous."

"It's Leigh, Polly."

"Still."

"We have to trust her. She let us have the clone," Julian said. "She wants you to monitor it."

"This is the craziest shit I've ever heard. Or imagined hearing, buy..." Frank lifted his glass. "To tomorrow night."

Polly refused, at first. "I'm not drinking to a really suck-worthy idea."

"It would be," Julian acknowledged, "if weren't Leigh." He gestured toward Polly with his glass.

She relented. "Okay, okay. It is really your ass. And you have lots of this really good vodka."

~ ~ ~

By the time Frank and Polly had left, it was late. Julian sat at the kitchen table for a while, trying to put his finger...

To divine...

... what Leigh was doing. Predictably, it was beyond him. He took the open bottle of Grey Goose and Valium upstairs to their bedroom. He knew the vanity had several Valium bottles, but the kitchen bottle was already open. He was not sure he was up to any extra effort.

He settled against the bolster on his side of the bed – Leigh's remained in place, for symmetry, he had told himself – legs stretched out. He balanced the laptop on his thighs. He poured himself first two fingers of the vodka. It looked pathetic, so poured a thumb's worth more.

"Can it be that only the Triple-*V* can grant insight into another plane?" he mused aloud. "Oops. We're a V short. Maybe, later."

The Lily icon disappeared. A new, different Lily icon appeared. It was the same photo, just reversed. "Well, that's a mirror image." Dumbly stating the obvious sounded vaguely drunk. He had the uncomfortable feeling he was reaching the wrong *other plane*.

His right hand slapped the Valium onto his bed stand and gave the vodka glass a gentle nudge away from him. He needed that hand for the touchpad and the mirrored Lily icon. He slowly navigated the cursor to the icon and circled it before it alighted on the flipped Lily.

He was not hesitating. He was asserting the little control he had. He was sure of what to do, and he did it.

He tapped the touchpad.

The tiny Lily disappeared in favor of Excel and Lily's List.

His certainty vanished.

The contents were different, similar, but modified. The familiar table showed different values. He had memorized the earlier ones. His eyes had missed the main difference at first. Leigh had rewritten the note in the spanning cell at the top. It was for him, *about* him.

For My Dearest Julian,
This Lily's List is for you to follow.
I know how hard it will be.
But it is important to follow each step just right.
It is the only way.
Don't forget to enter your current weight.
Dosage is critical.
Don't forget to set your tolerance level.
2 should do it,
but you will have to decide.

PS: I'm going to try a video.
To tell you something new.
Something too hard to say out loud or write here.
I was a little ashamed. I should be.
Now, I'm not. Not at all.
I know you will understand my message.

Love, eternally (And I will prove it)

Leigh

The differences in the note stunned him, initially. Then he became intrigued.

What do you want?

The note was still directed to him, but, it had changed: It was for him. The phrases *current* weight and *your* tolerance level made that much clear. Julian ran his eyes up and down to the table. On her heaviest day, Leigh weight one hundred twenty-five. The number he recalled from her last entry had been 91 pounds. The number in weight cell was 190, a decent estimate of his own reduced weight.

"Oh."

Julian typed in 91. The dosage numbers plummeted. He entered 150. The numbers increased. He reentered 190 and let the dosage return to what she had sent him.

His.

His eyes went to the tolerance level and put in 3, instead of 2.

The calculations are for me.

His stupor evaporated with that realization. Leigh. She *was* definitely sending him a message.

For My Dearest Julian.

This is how you reach me.

She had laid it all out She had been a little coy, perhaps, but he finally got what should have been obvious all along. His denial had blocked it.

He may not have known *what* it was about. He did not know the why. He knew for sure *when.*

Now, I know how.

Julian sprung out of bed and hurried to the steps. He stopped and looked at the angel. He understood why he had not been able to store it or the others. They belonged.

He continued to the cellar. When purchasing the LCD TV, he had added a long HDMI cord to connect it to Leigh's laptop. The TV had no wifi or networking software. He had used the cable only once, to test it Leigh had refused the have an ugly black cord bisecting their bedroom.

"When you will trip on it going to the bathroom, I'll have to scold you. I don't want to do that."

He had kept it in his top dresser drawer for all of three days until Leigh found it attached to one of his tennis socks.

It had lived in the cellar ever since, in the space behind where the angels' boxes were supposed to be.

It took a few minutes, but he found the HDMI cable. He checked to be sure both plugs were undamaged. He calmed himself and forced slow steps up the two flights of stairs. Once in their bedroom, he threw the cable onto the bed. He took one end to the TV, angled the TV and secured one HDMI connector into the back of the TV. He noted that the HDMI input was port number three. He left the TV angled in case he had to redo the connection.

He kept almost comical control of himself, under the circumstances. He stepped over to his side of the bed...

As if on eggshells.

Oh, of course.

He positioned himself and put the laptop on his thighs, sideways. He plugged in the HDMI cable.

He turned on the TV with its own remote and navigated to *Settings* and the *Input Selection Menu*. He picked *Input 3*. The laptop screen leaped onto the TV, a distorted version of its three-minute slow aqua clock file prominent in the right corner.

"Whatever you've planned, you are the lead, Leigh. Only full-screen HD will do you justice," he said, although the laptop screen was compressed on the TV. "I'll get it right." It took him less than a minute to adjust to the widescreen dimensions of the laptop. The screen's corner clock was finally round. "See. If you give me a second chance, I will get it right."

He disconnected the HDMI from the laptop, rose and stowed the cable behind the dresser, still attached to the TV. He sat back down on the bed.

"To tomorrow night," he said, toasting with his vodka. "To second chances."

Chapter Eighteen

August 19, 2013

Julian inspected his kitchen. He pulled out Leigh's bag of pill bottles and set it between the laptop and the TV. He would deal with them later. He had already started the preliminary doses on Lily's List and had yet to feel a hint of a buzz.

Tolerance level adjustment?

He had taken pain meds over the years for back pain and diazepam for leg cramps at night. Of course, he had an excellent tolerance level when it came to alcohol.

He checked his Rado watch. A few of his collection had digital displays, but they were not accurate. The Rado had sweep hand and a digital display to hundreds of a second. He spent half an hour getting it to match the laptop's exact lag. The kitchen clocks would wait. He had a plan to go room by room.

Next to the little TV, a set of keys dangled from the deadbolt porch door reminded him of two things: How clever he had been to install an inside-outside keyed deadbolt, and there was another key.

As he went to unlock the door, he checked his appearance in the upper frames of the door's windows. He no longer looked entirely homeless. He had showered and washed his hair but used his electric razor with its stubble setting. Not that he bought into the current *Actor Look*, but because

Leigh had last seen him that way. He did not know what was coming, but matching that last day seemed in everyone's best interest.

He wore the same clothes, too, though those needed a dryer run with anti-stat sheets to remove a year's dust.

Outside, he again looked around, taking in the whole porch like a long-lost acquaintance. He had barely used it in the last year. The grill, the chaises and their tables, the bistro, set all sat with varying layers of crusts of dust and pollen.

The point of the visit, however, was Leigh's *lunatic angel.* It was the most frightening thing they owned... excluding the laptop, of course. He approached it with his index fingers crossed. He had often done that, always eliciting a laugh from Leigh.

Today, I mean it.

When the angel did not leap at him, he tilted her head forward and removed the spare key.

Frank and Polly had promised to stay out of it, but they were such good friends with the best of intentions.

The best locks make the best friends.

After he had returned to the kitchen, he laid the angel's key on the counter. He had forgotten something. He looked at the key laying next to the TV.

What?

"Oh. Now that would be dumb."

He pocketed the keys hanging in the inside lock.

Break a window pane, Frank? Forget it.

No point in getting all cut up.

He realized he was missing something, else. His mind was a little fuzzier than he had thought. Something about breaking the window floated in the back of his mind.

The chairs.

He took the keys from his pocket, unlocked the deadbolt and reentered the porch. One at time moved the bistro chairs out of the way in the dining room. The chaises and the tables went into the angels' lair. He hefted the bistro table. It was heavy and awkward, but Frank was strong enough to lift it high enough to poke the glass in the porch door.

Julian lugged the table into the living room.

That left nothing on the porch except the grill. He removed the grates and put them on the bistro table. Satisfied, he returned to the kitchen, locked the door and pocketed the keys again. He went into the dining room and living room. Both rooms looked like hell.

Sorry, precautions come first.

He returned to the kitchen and descended the steps to the basement.

As an essential part of his bizarre plan – bizarre but not sure-fire, he admitted – from the ground up, he would set the whole house back in time, by three minutes.

As he went, he had the nagging feeling he had missed something obvious.

~ ~ ~

For hours, Erin battled herself. It was the one-year anniversary of Leigh's death. She had seen Julian at that one lunch day, and she knew she had to go to Julian. She had committed herself to Leigh... well, to Julian, to both.

To me.

On the other hand, she did not want to force anything or to intrude on his grief. In his fragile state, he might reject her completely. Such damage might take forever to repair.

I can wait, but I promised.

She had awakened to it – her own grief – as if the one-year anniversary opened the door to it. She struggled with brutal sobs minute by minute during the day. She had called in sick, not fooling her supervisor at Renegade's, who told her to take the week.

Erin hoped more than anything that Julian would call her. She knew he would not. She hoped Frank or, more likely, Polly would and implore her to go. She had picked up her cell dozens of time to call either or both of them. She tried to sleep. She tried to awaken.

Finally, late afternoon, she got out of bed again, changed her clothes and looked in the mirror. Her hair was ratty, her complexion graded from sallow to positively ruddy. Her eyes were worse, swollen and with red highlights. She left the bathroom crying.

Her apartment was too small for effective pacing. She considered eating as a distraction and ended up barely to the bathroom sink, puking half on herself.

That settles it.

If Julian or anyone else needs me, he doesn't need me looking like yesterday's zombie.

Erin took a hot shower of indeterminate length scrubbing herself, washing and conditioning her hair. She rarely did the latter. She stood under the sub-scalding water until she could not stand waiting. After toweling off, she put a touch of gel in her hair and blew it dry, two more things she did only occasionally.

Pleased with her hair, she took on the stranger's face in the mirror.

First came the *Visine* eye de-reddener. She had used the eye-drops for years – what with boyfriends who came and went, never measuring up – but had squirted gallons in the last year.

Can one OD from eye-drops?

From the looks of things, maybe I have.

Her complexion had improved to the extent that it was an even red from the shower. She rinsed it with cold water until it approximated normal and walked out of the bathroom. She had to take a moment to consider her *look.*

She paced to the extend the apartment allowed. It was crucial that she look... appropriate. The day was not one for dolling up, not something she felt she ever could. It was a day for mourning.

Leigh?

It was the day for starting over.

Back to the bathroom, she went. She applied a respectful level of make-up – she always worried about her limited touch with makeup – just some blush, a touch of mascara, fine eyeliner and subdued lipstick. There was no point in covering the freckles that made her look too young.

I'm not too young.

She chose slim-cut ivory slacks over her familiar skinny jeans. Even she knew the slacks showed off her hips and legs nicely. She picked a light green camisole, to accent her hazel eyes with a suitable black linen top button more than half way up. Her shoes were the simple black, two-inch pumps she had worn the last time she had seen Julian.

She had worn them with the outlandish hope that Frank might bring Julian with him. The truth was that she carried those pumps to work in a big purse every day for a year.

For a minute or two, she examined herself in the mirror. She was convinced Leigh would give her a signal if the *look* was too far off. Instead of a negative vibe, she kept feeling better about herself and her mission.

Erin drove slowly – but resisted urges for U-turns – until she reached the front of their... Julian's house. Flashing back to her last hug with Leigh, she could not bring herself to pull into the driveway. She had the *Visine* handy and waited until the crying stopped to use it again. She delayed further until the drops had done their magic.

The inventor must have suffered love and loss once too often.

No one wants to believe someone else wept more deeply.

She hit the steering wheel, just hard enough to stop thinking. She got out of the car and began the long walk up Julian's driveway.

~ ~ ~

Julian sat on the love seat in the finished game room, the laptop next to him. He focused on focusing. His varying concentration concerned him. He had a lot of preparing to do.

They had not used the room much, but it had a full array of TV gear, all of it on at that moment. The cable box allowed no adjustment from Comcast's transmission of the time. It did have a manual setting to prevent the display of the time and Julian used it. He set the TV to correct less three minutes. He did the same with the DVD player. He left them on and left the basement.

Then he turned around and went back to the Comcast box. Its display showed the date only.

But you disagree, don't you?

Julian felt ridiculous, but he could not help but think the cable box was subversive. He unplugged it.

To be sure, Julian was not sure that anything failing to display the *correct* wrong time would foul up Leigh's plan, but he was not taking any chances.

In the kitchen, he manually set the clocks on the microwave, the oven and the TV to the laptop time, to minute, the best he could do. The simple, low-rent Comcast box did not display time, as did the larger ones in the bedroom and basement, but he knew it was getting the time from Comcast. He pulled its plug.

There!

Everything including *the kitchen sync.*

As he walked through the opening to the dining room, Julian halted.

Damn!

The wall land-line had a tiny time display. Julian reached for it and tried to find a way to change the time, without success. Resigned, he pulled the phone out of the wall.

Who uses landlines, anyway?

Then he saw that the microwave ticked a minute ahead of the stove's clock.

That wasn't going to fucking work.

Julian unplugged both appliances and killed their offending clocks.

Thank God, the fridge is timeless.

I hate warm vodka.

At that moment, Julian had realized that no clock was better than an *offending* clock. He raced downstairs and yanked all the cords out of the sockets. Figuratively mocking the plan, the front-running Comcast box crashed to the floor. He had not touched it.

Julian kicked the box all the way to the garage passage door.

It felt good to give Comcast the boot.

Still, he hoped he had not broken it. Getting a replacement would be a pain.

~ ~ ~

Unlike Julian and his porch, Frank and Polly used their deck most summer days for early evening cocktails, unless Julian or someone showed up with a haunted laptop. For the last year, the cocktail hour(s) had centered on worrying about Julian, but not like August 19, 2013.

The clone slept on a table to Frank's right.

"We should be with him," Polly said. "This isn't right. Even without all the cloning nonsense."

"I agree, but he doesn't want us there. It's his deal, Polly."

"One way or another, this day may kill him."

"Not if you're right. Not if it's Leigh."

"Maybe, she'll see how fragile he is and come to her senses."

"Assuming it is not simply Julian's mind playing tricks with him and with Leigh's laptop–"

Polly glared at him, "Fuck you. And you don't believe that."

Frank looked back.

"Do you?"

"The alternative scares the hell out of me," he said.

~ ~ ~

Having returned to the kitchen, Julian opened the bag of pill bottles. Between those upstairs and in the kitchen, he knew he had enough for the Leigh's recipe ten times over, even at his body weight; however, many of the bottles bore five-year-old labels. She had hoarded the medications like they were angels.

Did they have enough oomph left?

The pills, not the angels.

Angels were all oomph. And cardboard, of course.

He had to pick out the newest refills.

Leigh had gone through a great many more pills the last three months of her life, increasingly so, than she had the previous months. At that point, she was always up to using the oldest pills first. The bottles in the kitchen got the least use.

He had warned her: Rotate the Stock.

He had done his best to help in that way, but the stress of need usually overcame reading. Perhaps, she had taken the declining strength of the Vicodin and Valium into account, as well as the tolerance to them. The Xanax played only a minor role in the recipe and screwed up the alteration and the Triple-V trademark. Leigh had not resisted the idea of the outlying Xanax but finally included it in the recipe. Though she had not nailed down its effect on her anxiety, she took it, and included it, to cover her bets.

He should have needed it, but anxiety had given way to anticipation: He was looking forward to the three minutes, in the craziest, clearly manic, way.

He threw the bottles aside from the Valium, Vicodin and Xanax in the sink.

It suddenly occurred to him, that Xanax had not made the cut for the final sequences, not in *his* Lily's List. He tossed it in the sink, as well.

You know me, don't you?

He opened the freezer. He had three fifths of Grey Goose, only one them cracked for a pair of three-ounce lunch portions.

Speaking of tolerance.

He had plenty. He pulled out the open bottle, got a tumbler and poured a few inches...

Pour a hand!

You don't have to drink it.

But you might.

He compared the bottles of Valium – or in most cases the generic, diazepam, but who called it that? – found the oldest and dumped them in the sink. He found one bottle from Spring 2012 and shook out about four. Tempted as he was to hurry things along, Leigh had a plan for him, part of which was to guarantee he had his wits about him. He pitched two and took out an eighteen-month-old Vicodin. He gagged them down with two ounces of the vodka.

How to ruin good vodka.

He rinsed his mouth with a bit of Grey Goose and spit it on top of the discarded bottles. He followed with a decent sip and felt better... for both himself and the Goose.

Suddenly, the loudest sound of the last week jarred him. He dropped the glass. "Fuck!"

He pulled out his cell phone and almost threw against a wall. It was not the phone.

The clanging came again.

Frank and Polly.

Go away, please.

"Go away, seriously," he called toward the front door. "Not you," he said to the Grey Goose bottle. "In fact, get to work." He got another glass and filled it halfway. He looked down at the cell phone. It displayed the correct time or the incorrect time under Julian's plan. He snapped off the back and removed the battery. He set both next to the angry angel head's key.

The distorted voice mimicked the Egg timer, said. "Julian?"

Erin.

"Shit." He went half way to the door, stopping in the dining room.

"Can I talk to you, please."

Not really.

It's not a year.

I'm keeping track.

Still, it was her voice, in some form, that Leigh had wanted him to hear for almost a year.

Oh, that plan.

Does it still count?

He went to the door and cracked it a few inches.

"Hi," she said, her voice all throaty and awkward. "Hi."

Julian felt a wave of appreciation breaking over the riptide of revulsion. Before long, he would be seasick. The riptide though was all him, not Erin.

She looked great, and he was too happy to see that she looked great. He wanted her to lift him out of whatever had happened to him.

Maybe later.

That plan had to wait.

Until next year.

He opened the door halfway, conceding to the half of him that wanted her to come in. The other half said, "Not a good time, Erin." He blurted out a laugh that surprised them both. "I mean, really. Not the right time."

She looked stricken by the laugh, his woozy look or the vodka odor or, more likely, all three. She pulled herself together, and the effort showed visibly. "I thought you might need a friend. You know, tonight."

"It's not that kind of night."

"But–"

"Erin, listen... I'm sorry, it isn't the time."

"I know. Maybe, tomorrow?"

Julian smiled, in spite of himself. "I believe that was that plan."

Her expression revealed she knew precisely what he meant. "So, you know I have my orders," she said, trying to be light.

"We all have our orders."

"What about Frank and Polly? Are they–"

"They are otherwise occupied."

That brought a flash of anger. "Doing what, for Christ fucking sake?"

He held out his palm. "No. It's not them," he began, cutting himself off before he revealed too much. Just seeing her there made him want to tell her, but that was not the current plan.

"I asked them to work on something for me," he said. "Just not here."

"Oh," she said, mollified. "But you shouldn't be alone. Not tonight."

Julian smiled. "Would it help if I said…" He raised both eyebrows. "I won't really be alone?"

Erin shocked them both by smacking him lightly on the chest and leaving hand there. She gave him a push. "Great. Scare the rest of the shit out me."

"I meant Memories, Erin." The lie sounded convincing.

"Okay. If you're sure?"

"It's my best guess."

She turned to go but turned back. "Call me. If you need me," she said, trying to hold his eyes. She could not quite pull it off, as they both looked away. "I mean it. I can't sleep."

"You should be out with your boyfriend. Living it up." He hopped a little and instantly regretted the attendant lightheadedness. He did not stick the landing.

She reached for him, but he took an unsteady step away.

The rejection made her angry. "It's not just you, you cruel mother-fucker," she snapped. Her eyes got huge in horror. When they closed, they squeezed out some tears. "I'm so sorry. It's just… I loved her, too. And you. Don't you know that?"

Those simple truths irked him. He was angry at himself. He was angry at Leigh and her damned plans. Others were affected, too, and he missed it in his own self-indulgence. "I know, Erin," was the best he could do. He added, "I've been kind of crazy."

Her eyes softened. "Besides… I haven't had a boyfriend for over a year."

"So, I'm not the only crazy guy out there."

She pointed to her chest and smiled a little. "Include one girl."

"Well," Julian said, realizing the conversation had to end, or he would fall behind schedule. "Tomorrow, we can swap crazy stories."

She brightened further. "Really? That would be... nice."

"Don't be so sure. I'm planning on winning."

"It isn't a contest," she said.

"Oh, I know. And I will prove it."

"Is that a promise? Tomorrow, I mean?"

"Pretty close. It may be a long night. Yes, it's a promise."

"Okay." She pulled out her cell phone and hit the speed-dial number for Julian's cell. She had gotten the number from Julian, ages ago, allowing her to get updates on Leigh – and Julian – without bothering Leigh directly. Her phone rang to his voice mail. "There. You have my number now."

"Where do I rank?" he asked. "On the speed-dial."

"Sorry. Number nine." She kissed him hard on the cheek. "Call me, please. Tonight, I mean. Even if you just want to hear a friendly voice. "

He laughed. He heard her friendly *Oh, Julian* a lot. "I will," he lied. "It was nice of you to stop by. I was a little slow in showing it, but I appreciate it. Tomorrow."

"Tomorrow. Bye."

Julian waved when she looked back from the driveway. He missed her presence for a moment, steeled his resolve and dead-bolted that door, too.

If she came back later – and he just knew she would – Julian would have to ignore her. He hated that idea. He looked out the dining room window as she looked up one last time.

He closed the blind.

~ ~ ~

They all knew that Leigh's official time of death was 10:12 PM, August 19, 2012. It was not like Julian had noted the exact time, but later, he did work back from the Egg timer to figure the 10:12. However, if the files meant anything, Leigh had died at exactly 10:12, not a hundredth of a second one way or the other.

As 10:00 PM approached, Polly was pacing, increasingly frazzled. She kept eyeing the minutes passing on her iPhone. She could not look at the clone. "We can still get over there."

Frank was not much better, but he was sitting, his eyes on the clone. There still was no egg timer. He had not brought himself to reopen Lily's List, but the time had come. "Wait a second, Pol. This shit has changed completely. The weight, the doses."

Polly rushed over and bent over. She dropped to a crouch when she noticed the layout of the text at the top of the page. "Holy... The note, Frank. The one at the top."

"What?"

"She changed it. She says it's for Julian, not her."

Frank read the note. He did not have to read it twice, probably could not have read it twice. The words spilled out his mouth. "She's nuts." He could not believe he had completely given in. "What is she doing? She can't want him to do this."

"No? No, I don't..." Polly struggled for clarity. "The video. She'd never do that. She wants him to see the video!"

"What can it possibly say that justifies making him follow this. He won't make to any video. This is a suicide plan, Polly. That's what is has always been."

"Oh, God."

"Call him," Frank said. "Let me check the video."

Polly hit a speed dial key for Julian's land-line line and then the speaker key. The phone just rang and rang. "Damn him! He must have canceled his landline's voice mail." She ended the call.

"Frank had the clone's ftp screen up. It had not changed. The video file was firmly on only the web column. "Try his cell."

She hit another speed dial. The phone rang and went to voicemail. "No dice."

"Fuck him. Let's go." Frank got up and grabbed the clone.

"We have no chance."

The ring of Frank's cell phone stopped them both. "Thank God," Polly said, collapsing into a chair.

"Julian? Why have you–"

"No. Frank. Hi. It's Erin." She sounded panicked. "I'm here. He won't talk to me. I know he can hear me."

"Erin? What–"

"Erin?"

"She's there," Frank said. "I think she got Julian on the phone."

"Really?"

Frank took a breath. "Erin. You're saying he's on the phone. We–"

"No, I'm here. At the front door. He was loopy when I was here. Earlier. I think he was drunk. He'll get depressed." Her voice sped on. "Then I called, but he wouldn't answer. So, I came back. He saw me. I know he did. I saw him. In a window. He shut the blinds. I thought he'd come down–"

"He's in the middle of something," Frank said.

"What something? No, I don't care!" Erin gulped for breath. "But he looked wrong. He shouldn't be alone. He saw me! He closed the blind!"

Polly took Frank's hand in her right and used her left to gesture palm down. "We all have to calm down, she whispered in his ear."

"Calm down, Erin." He muted the phone. "What in the fuck do I tell her?"

Polly thought, for approximately two nanoseconds. "She has to get inside. That's all there is to it. She's there. We're not."

Frank nodded. "Erin? On the porch. There is a key–"

"The evil angel! Yes, yes! I know!"

~ ~ ~

Her cell glued to her ear, Erin backed away from Julian's front door. She ran down the steps and across the driveway. She began up the stairs as fast as she could. She stumbled and dropped her phone onto the driveway. The back popped out, but the battery stayed in. She hurried down to reclaim it. She snapped the back on. "Frank? Are you still there?

"Yes. What happened?'

"I dropped the phone. The battery stayed–" She looked at her battery indicator. "Shit. My cell battery is low. I'll call back when I've got the key." She turned off the phone and put it her slack's pocket.

She mounted the step, two at time. When she reached the porch, she stopped dead in her tracks. Everything was gone, except the grill. There was one other thing.

"Hi, angel. Where's you plant?"

She turned on her phone.

~ ~ ~

As Julian surveyed his handiwork, his desktop and table matched the laptop all displayed 9:54, August 19, 2013. He had put the tablet into airplane mode so that he could set its time manually.

He went into the second bedroom. He looked at his battery-operated clock on a bedside table. It received a signal that kept it at what he came to call the *incorrect* time. He pulled out the batteries and threw it in the closet.

He was behind schedule. By reflex, he looked at the Rado, and it hit him. He strode to the watch drawer, pulled it open and looked at the dozen watches. He picked up his silver Wittnauer to reset it. He knew the Rado was properly adjusted, but... He ran to get the laptop. It was the only official timepiece of the night. He set the Wittnauer to 9:55.

The laptop turned over to 9:56. The Wittnauer did not.

"This is not going to work."

~ ~ ~

"This is a kill list, Polly," Frank said, shaking his head at the clone's Lily's List. "It had Leigh's weight the first time. This little blue cell is Julian's."

"She wouldn't do that."

"You know I'd say it was Julian, that he did it, but... I guess he could have rewritten the note–"

"No way. It's not him."

"So, Leigh wants to kill him?" Frank had an idea he should have had earlier. He checked the properties of Lily's List. The result shocked him. "The file isn't read-only, but all the gray cells are locked, including the text. There should be a password to undo it, but..."

"But?"

"There isn't. I'm not sure I could edit this file."

"Meaning? Come on, Frank," Polly snapped. "Don't fuck with me, now, asshole!"

"Meaning, I'm all in, now. In Leigh-land. But I don't know what *she's* doing.

Her energy draining, Polly pressed her eyelids. "Please, please, Erin."

~~ ~

Erin said, "Frank. I'm here."

Before approaching the angel, Erin strode over to the kitchen door and looked through the four-pane window. What she saw clenched at her heart. There are pill bottles and an empty vodka bottle in the sink. "Oh, Julian."

"What, Erin? What?" Frank asked.

Glued to the spot, Erin said, "There are pill bottles. Lots. In the sink."

"We don't have to worry about those."

"What is he doing?'

Erin heard Frank whisper, "Should I tell her?"

Polly whispered back, "She has to know. Right fucking now!"

"What? Tell me what? Not about these? What do you mean."

"There are other pills."

"Okay?"

"He's going to use them," Frank said. "A lot of them."

~ ~ ~

Julian had the entire drawer of watches in their bedroom., sitting on Leigh's dresser. He opened the window. And began to throw them outside, one at a time, in no hurry. He had a minute or two to spare. The first couple landed on the porch roof. Once he reevaluated the distance and his arm, he got the third over the roof. It was his prized Wittnauer.

"Julian!" he heard. The Egg's voice, he was pretty sure.

~ ~ ~

Erin felt relief when she heard a window open above her.

The next pinging sound surprised her, then the second. She backed away from the door and walked off the porch.

"Julian!"

"Back to Switzerland," she heard Julian say.

Something whizzed past her head. She looked down at the silver watch on the ground, just as a second watch hit her shoulder. She stepped away, under cover of the roof, as another hit where she had been standing.

"He's throwing watches out the window," she reported.

On the other end, there was silence. Then, Frank said, his voice kind of hollow. "He can't sync them. They're the wrong time."

"Is he crazy, Frank?" she asked, terrified of the answer. "He didn't seem... right."

"Believe it or not, Erin," Polly said, "if he is, so are we. He thinks it's Leigh."

Frank said, "We don't know. It doesn't matter. Get the key. Get in there!"

Erin went over to the angry angel. She tilted its head. She felt for the key. The compartment felt empty. She yanked the head off the wall and dug into the back.

"It's not here! The key, Frank." She carried the angel head to the door, stunned. She looked inside, using several different angles. She finally saw a cell phone, a battery, and a key. She staggered back, unbalanced by the weight of the angel until she hit the grill. If there had been a chair, Erin would have fallen into and disintegrated under the weight of the angel. "He took it. He took the key! I can't get in."

~ ~ ~

In their bedroom, the watch drawer was on the floor, in the far corner. The Comcast box sat on the floor, blank. The DVD player, sat next to, also powerless. The TV was on, to a blue screen, the HDMI cable plugged in. The cable drooped toward the bed and snaked to the laptop in the middle of the mattress. Julian had not yet plugged it into the laptop. The TV remote sat on the laptop's keyboard.

To the right of the bed, on Julian's bedside table, sat two large Vicodin bottles and two small Valium bottles, one of each open. Three shot glasses sat empty next to the bottles.

On the laptop's screen, the revised Lily's List sat in its window. The cursor blinked in the *weight* cell, which still read 190.

Julian looked it all over, standing in their bathroom door, dressed as he had been exactly one year earlier. He ducked in and stepped on the scale. Earlier in the day, he had established the weight of his clothes at 4.6 pounds. The scale read 187.8.

"Not my favorite diet," he said to Leigh.

He left the bathroom and sat on Leigh's side of the bed and looked at the laptop, waiting. For what, he did not know.

Something told him he belonged on his side of the bed. He was not sure.

Give me another message.

Just a little sign.

As if in answer, Egg and its count-down clock popped open all by itself. Erasure's *When Will I See You Again* began to play.

"I can't argue the choice," Julian said, "but I was expecting Maroon 5, again." He checked the laptop time. It was 10:03:10 PM. "I guess not."

At first, he was so surprised by the music and the dancing that he did not notice the new angel icon. The one resting quietly above the text *Video.me.mp4*.

~~~
~~~

Frank and Polly stared at the laptop. The egg was dancing to *When Will I See You Again* on the clone. At first, that was all they could do.

"That song," Frank said, in disbelief, or, rather, in belief. "Is she kidding?"

Polly's voice was barely audible. "Forget the song. It's the video–"

"What song?" Asked Erin over the phone. After a hesitation, she cried, "You're playing the same song!"

"Frank cloned Leigh's laptop," Polly explained. "So, yes. Can you hear it both places?"

"Yes, yes. I don't understand. Is this Leigh?"

"We think so," Frank said, his eyes still fixed on the angel icon for the video.

Polly muted the phone. "There's only time for the last song. After this one's done."

"Jesus Christ."

She unmuted the phone. "Erin, whatever you have to do, you *have* to get in there."

"I don't have the key!" Erin started to cry, pounding the heavy angel head on the top of the grill. "You stupid, fucking, heavy thing!"

~ ~ ~

Julian wobbled back into the bedroom with a new, frosty Grey Goose bottle. Earlier, he had begun the preliminaries earlier, pills, glasses – one was for water for the pills; now way either of them could consider taking all the pills with even a vodka as smooth as Grey Goose – and the vodka. Leigh had laid it all out for him.

Leigh had omitted one specification, *i.e.*, where he was supposed to being laying during the Lily's List ritual.

He had assumed he would lay in his usual spot, but that seemed wrong. She had been in her usual position, so it made sense for him to copy her. Besides, to be closer to her, he should have occupied her space. What if she wanted... to occupy her space?

Figuratively. Right?

This is your specialty.

He tried to think of it from her point of view. When they were together on the bed, they had always been Leigh on the left and Julian on the left... depending on how one looked at it. Lily's List was no for him, not her so that fact argued for his side.

He looked to the laptop for advice. There it sat: The video.

In the video, they had been shoulder-to-shoulder, she on the left, he on the right.

Done.

He saved precious seconds, to boot.

The countdown hit one minute. He wondered if Leigh would stick with Elvis. He assumed so, but he had assumed Maroon 5, too and gotten *When Will I See You Again*.

He sat in his spot, as usual, against the bolster, his legs stretched out.

Half a minute was left in the song.

It was time to seat the laptop for its video performance. He balanced it on his thighs. He plugged in the HDMI. The TV exploded with the laptop's screen.

Satisfied, Julian entered his new net weight into the weight cell in Lily's List. The dosage numbers refreshed, changing slightly.

"It's official," he said. "That's a paltry dose of vodka." He drank one of the vodka's and refilled the glass.

He reached for the two bottles and poured out a bunch of Valium. He returned some, leaving the correct amount in his hand. He angled the Vicodin bottle and took the required number. "Ready?" He tossed them in the air... and onto the sheet.

"That's either too much prep work," he said, "or a mixed signal."

He hurriedly gathered up the pills. Egg danced the countdown to ten seconds. It looked spooky big on the TV.

He heard the Egg voice call his name a little early and he looked in its direction. It was too far away to matter.

"Ding! Oh, Julian! That voice came from his lap.

The video bloomed, along with Elvis.

"*There* you are."

~ ~ ~

Before Elvis started, Polly and Frank could hear Erin call out, "Julian!" Polly and Frank were distracted by the phone and they almost missed what happened at the same instant that *I Can't Help Falling* began on the clone.

A video window popped open, with a pale version of Leigh.

"This is the video," Polly said. "This is what she was talking about."

Leigh began.

Polly said, "Dear God, Frank."

Frank was mesmerized by Leigh's weak, gravelly voice.

> *You know, Julian, you may never see this video.*

Julian's voice could be heard from the kitchen, the words indistinct. Her face ran through several expressions, but the impression was conflict.

> *You have under three–*

Leigh coughed suddenly. The cough sounded terrible and obviously scared her. She barely got the tissue to her mouth in time. She seemed calmed by the tissue's contents.

I'm not showing off my new expertise,
I'm practicing–"

Another cough, a deep one, interrupted her. She tried to contain with Kleenex.

She hid the surface of the tissue, but it bled through enough to show how dark the blood was. She balled it up and threw it away, with a *fuck you, I'm busy* look. She picked up new ones.

Or not. I'd better just say it.
I can delete it later.

Doubt spread on her face. She had trouble talking. The next cough was a little worse. Still, she tried to smile.

This my first attempt at a last video for
you–

Her head dropped, and her arms flopped.

"I can't watch this," Polly said.

Leigh fought her way back.

Don't be disappointed in me.
It's because I love you too much.

"This may kill him," Polly said.

"But what does disappointed mean? In what's she's doing?"

"Erin!" Polly shouted into the phone.

~ ~ ~

Julian said, "Hi."

She was on the TV screen. He heard distant sounds of his name. All that mattered was in the room, but he did notice that the sounds stopped.

Leigh's voice was coming from the TV, too – and the laptop, perfectly in sync – pained, a whisper above a whisper. She looked so alone without him.

Where am I?

Julian, this is my first take.
While you're down in the kitchen.
For three minutes.

She laughed which brought another cough. She added something inaudible, ending with egg. She has very little of the raspy breath behind her word. The cough went into the tissue. She looked at it, her expression worried. She continued, halting after every few words to breathe.

I may not finish it, but that's okay.
You probably shouldn't see it... anyway.
Maybe later.
I'm putting it off. I have put off thinking it.
I have to say it out loud.
It will make me sound petty to you at first.
This is the only way I can.
I just love you... too damn much–

Leigh suppressed a cough and made a pale show of triumph. She cups her hand under her right ear and listened. Suddenly, her breathing cratered and her energy level dropped further. Her next breath was an attempt at a deep one. It rattled into a triple coughing attack, the sound of which she tried to contain.

Wow. That hurt.
I hope you don't hear... that downstairs.
You're easily distracted, sometimes.

She looked at the tissue.

More wow.
That doesn't look... like just blood anymore.

Julian nodded as knowingly as his deepening fog permits.

I thought this would be easy. Fun, even.
The video, I mean.
Not what I have to say. It's not. It's hard.
But I need to tell you.
So, you'll have to see me tell it.

It's hard to believe, but you were right all along.

Leigh's voice, her expressions, her presences seemed to noticeably fade.

"I'm here," Julian said, fading with her.

Leigh swung her right arm slowly toward Julian's side of the bed.

Hold my hand.

Julian reached his left for her hand.

That's it.

On screen, Leigh tightened her hand.

Julian did the same.

I love Erin.
It's not about her. It never was.

~ ~ ~

Elvis's voice from upstairs held Erin captive. She heard faint whispers, too, and her name! She heard her name!

"Julian?"

Polly's voice cut through. "Erin! You have to get to him!"

"I can't, I can't," Erin whined into the phone balanced.

"Break down the fucking door, if you have to!"

Erin turned toward the door, still holding onto the angel. She did not get far, but her phone slid to the porch floor

"Oh, Jesus." Erin had her instrument. She directed her anger and her desperation outward: She took two long strides and pitched the angel into the door's lower right window pane.

The angel flew straight into the glass and shattered the pane and its frame. The angel bounced to the ground.

The effect startled Erin but she recovered quickly. She retrieved her phone. "I broke the window!" she shouted.

She hefted the angel again and clear most of the glass still in the lower panes of the door. She dropped the angel on the ground to gain a few extra inches. She was tall enough to angle her shoulders and then her waist into the opening. Her hips were not going to make it. She ignored the remaining glass cutting into her and shoved the TV to the floor. Using the counter for support. She reached the key.

Still hanging, she unlocked the door from the inside.

That was dumb as shit!

She wriggled out and opened the door. "I'm in!"

A bloody mess, but in!

Not her best look for Julian.

Taken aback by her vanity, she hesitated.

"What do you see?" Polly demanded.

"Pills. Lots of pills Bottles."

She rooted through the pill bottles. "They're full. That's good? Right?"

~ ~ ~

Frank and Polly watched Leigh dying on the clone's screen. If it were not for the horrifying thought that Julian was following her, their hearts would have simply broken.

Instead, they heard Erin.

Frank finally spoke, "I doubt it. If he's upstairs, there are plenty more."

Erin took a few seconds. "Okay. Fuck."

On the clone, the screen tilted about ten degrees.

"Damn it, Julian," Polly said.

"It's not him, Pol. It's Leigh."

"Get upstairs, Erin!" Polly cried. "Run!"

~ ~ ~

Erin had no idea how much she had bled. She slipped and was saved by the refrigerator her own blood and landed on the kitchen floor. Her shoe slipped again. She kicked off her bloody pumps and bolted for the stairs.

~ ~ ~

Julian heard his own faint voice.

I'm almost there–

His voice. He remembered saying it, but it was time to say, then, "I'm with you, Leigh."

The truth surprised me, Julian.
That I love you too much.
Turns out that's... very possible.
I saw it on this screen.
There is no me and you.
It is only us.

"Wherever you need me to be." Julian's eyes closed. His hand clenched hers.

Elvis finished his singing, leaving only the piano.

~ ~ ~

Erin smashed the bedroom door open. She saw Julian. She saw Leigh. She saw their arms, their hands.

Julian's eyes opened slightly.

"Leigh! No!"

It's time, Julian.

As the last the last piano key of *I Can't Help Falling* reverberated, the image on the TV screen skewed completely, recording the original fall of Leigh's laptop.

"Don't Julian!" Erin begged. "I'm here!"

Julian closed his eyes, his hand tightened.

Instantly, the hands on the laptop/TV's aqua corner clock advanced three minutes, as did the companion digital time display and promptly disappeared.

The angel icon blinked away, and the screens flashed a particular shade of blue before fading to black.

~

Acknowledgments

The Last Three Minutes was inspired by a very real three-minute loss of laptop time. To this day, I do not know how it corrected itself. I could not fix it. My cousin Lynn Norman suggested it as the basis for a story. Everything else in the tale flowed from that real glitch.

(I thought the story would make a good screenplay. Obviously, I was wrong about that.)

In the Acknowledgment section for my epic 750-page novel *The Girl in the Coyote Coat,* I made the mistake of acknowledging the help of my sisters, Janet Nave and JoAnn Kiburz and friend Julie Kimball, for their alpha reading and editing assistance. Somehow, my compulsion to introduce two errors for every correction and rewrite they suggested may have made it impossible for them to get another similarly frustrating and non-paying gig.

So, other than the talented crew at Grammarly, *no one* helped me edit *The Last Three Minutes.* Besides, if anyone secretly did, they will never admit it.

About the Author

Born in 1950, John Nicholas Datesh lived mostly in and around Pittsburgh, Pennsylvania until early 2009. At Brown University, he took many courses in writing as an institutionalized rationale for doing just that. Then, at Boston University School of Law, he learned to mix in words and phrases like *It Depends* and *Hereinafter*. It is unknown when he learned to use italics every third paragraph.

In Spring 2009, he moved cats Lila and Lucy Liu to a condominium one mile in from the east side of Naples Bay in Florida. He left his Pittsburgh career in law, business and product development in favor of concentrating on writing fiction, winging blogs and cultivating beach chairs, presumably in that order of dedication.

He began writing fiction with a pencil and published, on paper with actual ink, his first three books, the SF/Mystery novel *The Nightmare Machine*; the Soft-boiled Detective novel *The Janus Murder*; and the International Suspense novel *The Moscow Tape*. All three novels are currently *evailable* in virtual ink at e-bookstores on the Web and in trade paperback.

Also widely *evailable* are the short stories *The Pro Station* (WWII), *The Final Equation (SF)* and *Reruns ad Infinitum* (SF/Fantasy). They join the author's definitive Christmas short story, *You Could Call It a Christmas Story* as works published after the move to Naples.

Shortly afer moving, he started up the humorous/satiric blog EmptyGlassFull.com. His short *Christmas Story* began as post to the blog, and he has e-published a collection its other early posts, grandly entitled *The Very First Blog Posts of All Time.* As novel writing began to take more of his time, he sent blogging on long vacation.

His 2013 novel, *The Girl in the Coyote Coat,* overran the boundaries of the mystery/suspense genre for which it was originally intended. No one would call it a romance, either. With a real estate and finance backdrop, the novel exposes the ways in which love, sex, money, scams, drugs, house-shopping/breaking and fur coats might affect the lives of complex and intriguing characters and even kill off a few.

2016's Sunset Noir mystery *The Body in the Bog* leads off the planned *Death by Condo* series starring prematurely retired lawyer Ian Decker.

His screenplay *The Last Three Minutes* was the first piece written partly on the beach and entirely in the Naples Bay scenery, though it is not set there. *The Last Three Minutes* has been adapted as a novel, if not a movie, by the author and was also published in 2016.

Author's Note on the novel *The Girl in the Coyote Coat* and *A Need Apart*

That heading is not an error. They are the same novel. So, why? To double sales? Not likely.

The novel *The Girl in the Coyote Coat* had a long, tortuous road to its final form, right down to the cover and the very title. It was published under that title after some serious consideration. The novel had gone through any number of working titles, as time allowed, from the 1979 original *The Real Estate Novel. The Girl in the Coyote Coat* was always my favorite, inspired, as it was, by an actual coyote coat on an actual model. In the end, that was the title I chose, in a close call (if only to me) over number two, *A Need Apart*, but I did not use the photo that initially inspired the title.

In 2016, I decided to experiment with some Amazon Kindle advertising. Amazon rejected the book's somewhat racy cover. That rejection got me thinking. The novel had grown into what I must loosely call a literary novel, if only because it does not fit into any genre. Why not try a different cover for an ad? Then, I thought, why not try a different, more literary-sounding title. The result is the identical novel with a different name, *A Need Apart*, and a different cover.

Ironically, the *A Need Apart*'s cover uses the shot that originally inspired the working title *The Girl in the Coyote Coat*. Fortunately, I love both titles and both covers, equally. Oh, and both the coat and model, too, if not quite so equally.

www.ingramcontent.com/pod-product-compliance
Lightning Source LLC
Chambersburg PA
CBHW020652030726
47498CB00002B/479